j616.3 SIL
Silverstein, Alvin.
Cystic fibrosis

JASPER COUNTY PUBLIC LIBRARY
Wheatfield Branch
Wheatfield, Indiana 46392

DEMCO

CYSTIC FIBROSIS

CYSTIC FIBROSIS

by Alvin, Virginia, and Robert Silverstein

A Venture Book
Franklin Watts
New York/Chicago/London/Toronto/Sydney

On the cover:
Micrograph of an alveolus, one of the microscopic air sacs of the lungs.

Photographs copyright ©: Wide World Photos: pp. 8, 73, 82; Custom Medical Stock Photo, Inc.: pp. 13 (Keith), 17 (DCRT/NIH), 25, 26 (CNRI/SPL), 33, 35 (Steinmark), 37 top and bottom right (Simon Fraser/RVI/SPL), 49 (SPL), 79 (Michael English, MD.); Photo Researchers, Inc.: pp. 20 (Petit Format/Nestle/SS), 30, 31 (both CNRI/SPL), 37 bottom left (Simon Fraser/ RVI/SPL); UPI/Bettmann Newsphotos: pp. 40, 58.

Library of Congress Cataloging-in-Publication Data

Silverstein, Alvin.
Cystic fibrosis / by Alvin, Virginia, and Robert Silverstein.
p. cm. — (A Venture book)
Includes bibliographical references and index.
ISBN 0-531-12552-1
1. Cystic fibrosis—Juvenile literature. [1. Cystic fibrosis.]
I. Silverstein, Virginia. II. Silverstein, Robert A. III. Title.
RC858.C95S55   1993
616.3'7—dc20   93-30045   CIP   AC

Copyright © 1994 by Alvin, Virginia, and Robert Silverstein
All rights reserved
Printed in the United States of America
6 5 4 3 2

CONTENTS

1
Cystic Fibrosis: A Deadly Inheritance
9

2
What Is Cystic Fibrosis?
11

3
How CF Affects the Body
15

4
Respiratory Problems
22

5
Digestive Problems
43

6
Other Body Systems
52

7
A Hereditary Disease
57

8
The Cystic Fibrosis Gene
65

9
The Testing Controversy
72

10
Future Treatment of Cystic Fibrosis
78

11
Gene Therapy: Hope for a Cure
89

12
Living with Cystic Fibrosis
95

Source Notes
98

Glossary
104

For Further Reading
108

Index
110

CYSTIC FIBROSIS

Allison Kay Brannon, a cystic fibrosis sufferer, was the 1975 National Poster Child for the Cystic Fibrosis Foundation. In the United States, four children a day are diagnosed with the disease.

1
CYSTIC FIBROSIS: A DEADLY INHERITANCE

When Jack Jacoby was sixteen, he asked his doctor, "I need to know how long I'm going to live, because I don't want to waste my parents' money going to college." Most teenagers don't think about things like that. But when Jack was three, doctors had told his worried parents that he had a disease called cystic fibrosis, or CF. At that time, in the late 1950s, a diagnosis of CF was practically a death sentence. In fact, most children with this disease died by the age of five or six. Jack's own sister, Jamie, had CF, too, and died when she was nine years old. Twice each day Jack had to have physical therapy to help him to breathe, and two years before he had been rushed to the hospital for an emergency operation. Could he really plan for the future now? Would he have the strength to finish not only four years of college but also medical school and the years of training needed to fulfill his dream of becoming a doctor?

"There's no way to really tell," Jack's doctor answered. "Just assume you're going to make it." He did, and went on to become a pediatrician, specializing in treating CF patients.[1]

Every day four children in the United States are diagnosed as having cystic fibrosis. CF is the most common inherited disease among Caucasians. Approximately one out of every two thousand Caucasian babies is born with it. (CF affects about one in seventeen thousand African-American babies and is even rarer in Orientals and Native Americans.)[2]

Of the four thousand diseases that are known to be inherited from our parents, cystic fibrosis is the number-one killer. Each day three people die from it.[3] But CF is no longer the nearly automatic death sentence it used to be. Improved treatments are allowing more than half of the people with CF to live into their mid-twenties, and some are already in their forties, fifties, and even sixties.[4]

Even with the improved treatments used today, living with CF is a long, never-ending struggle. But now, for the first time, medical researchers have hopes for a real cure for the disease. In the late 1980s scientists made a major breakthrough in the study of cystic fibrosis. They discovered the gene that causes the disease. In the few short years since that discovery, our understanding of CF has greatly increased. Although there is still a lot of work needed to bring a cure for cystic fibrosis, our better understanding of the disease is helping to keep the thirty thousand Americans who suffer from it healthier.[5] And there is hope that the young children today who have CF may live to see the time when no one will die from cystic fibrosis.

2
WHAT IS CYSTIC FIBROSIS?

You cannot catch cystic fibrosis from someone who has it. It is not a contagious disease. Instead, CF is a hereditary, or inherited, disease—a child is born with it. The symptoms usually begin at an early age, but they last throughout an entire lifetime.

The problems in CF start with thick, sticky mucus in the lungs and digestive system. This mucus builds up and clogs the breathing passages and the pancreas, an organ that produces digestive juices. The mucous plugs result in frequent lung infections and digestive problems. Over time the continual infections may cause the lungs and heart to weaken, until they are no longer able to function properly. Eventually the child may die.

HOW LONG HAVE DOCTORS KNOWN ABOUT CF?

References dating back to the 1600s describe children who probably had CF.[1] But doctors did not begin to think of CF as a separate disease until this century. One of the biggest reasons for this is that one of the major symptoms of CF—lung infections—was a common symptom of many other diseases, too. Another symptom—smelly, bulky stools—was also common to other illnesses. After antibiotics were developed, doctors noticed that some lung and gut infections did not seem to go away with treatment. The doctors began to suspect that something else was causing these continuing problems.

In 1936 Dr. Guido Fanconi of Switzerland described "cystic fibrosis of the pancreas" in children. In 1938 Dr. Dorothy Anderson at the Babies Hospital in New York City made the first thorough report of CF as a separate disease.[2]

In the early 1950s there was a heat wave in New York City, and doctors discovered that many of the children who were brought to hospitals for heat prostration were suffering from CF. This led one of Dr. Anderson's co-workers, P. A. DiSant'Agnese, to discover that people with CF had levels of salt in their sweat that were much higher than normal.[3] This discovery became the basis for the most accepted test to confirm a diagnosis of cystic fibrosis.

Until recently, cystic fibrosis was strictly a childhood disease. When CF was first described in the 1930s, nearly all children known to have the disease died within the first six months. But medical advances in diagnosis and treatment have helped patients to live longer. By the mid-1950s half of all children with CF died by the age of five. In 1966 half died before they were eleven. Today more than half the people born with CF live to be adults.

The pancreas, the organ directly behind the stomach, becomes congested with fibrous scar tissue and cysts in the disease that is named after this condition.

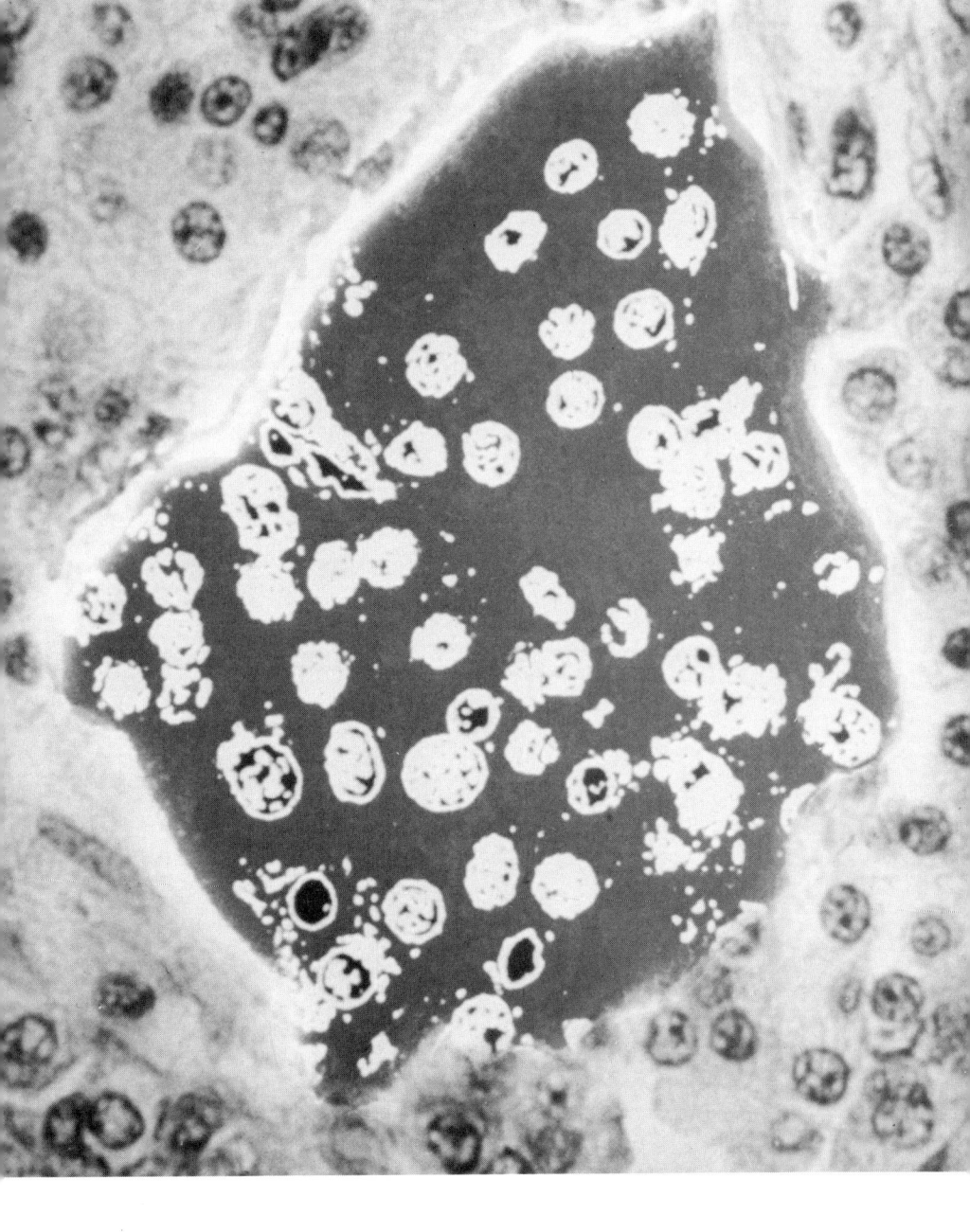

The average lifespan today for those with CF is twenty-nine.[4] But this average includes many who were born before doctors knew very much about CF. These patients are not able to benefit from many of the advances because their lungs have already been badly damaged. A child born with cystic fibrosis today may expect to live to forty or more—even without the new and exciting breakthroughs many experts are expecting in the near future.[5]

Many of the advances that have led to longer and healthier lives and a greater understanding of CF were made possible by the Cystic Fibrosis Foundation, organized in 1955 by a small group of families of CF patients. Today the foundation has more than 250,000 volunteers in more than seventy chapters. It supports a network of nearly 120 cystic fibrosis care centers across the United States. In addition to providing specialized care for CF patients, many of these centers are involved in pioneering research on this disease.

HOW DID CYSTIC FIBROSIS GET ITS NAME?

The pancreas is one of the places in the body where cystic fibrosis causes damage. It is an important organ that manufactures two different kinds of compounds: hormones, which travel through the bloodstream and act as chemical messengers; and enzymes, which help digest our food. Cystic fibrosis causes healthy tissue in the pancreas to be replaced by *fibrous* scars and fluid-filled cavities called *cysts*.

Cystic fibrosis is also sometimes called *mucoviscidosis*. This name comes from the fact that one of the major symptoms of the disease is thick and sticky (viscid) mucus in the lungs and digestive system.

3
HOW CF AFFECTS THE BODY

Something was wrong with baby Brianna. When her parents tickled her, she coughed instead of laughing. When she tried to cry, she gagged as if she was choking. And she was always sick. A cold would lead to pneumonia or bronchitis, and antibiotics didn't work as well as they should. She wasn't gaining weight, either. When she was a year old, she weighed less than she had at six months! The doctors didn't know what was wrong until a chest X ray showed that her lungs were filling up with thick mucus. Brianna had cystic fibrosis.[1]

CF AFFECTS THE EXOCRINE GLANDS

Cystic fibrosis causes *exocrine* glands in the body to work improperly. Exo means "out of," and these glands secrete fluids outward through tiny tubes called ducts, out to the surface of the body or into hollow organs such as the lungs and the intestines. Sweat glands, for example, pour watery sweat out onto the skin, and digestive juices produced in the pancreas flow through ducts into the intestines. Mucus, saliva, and tears are also exocrine secretions. All of these secretions are normally thin and slippery.

Other glands, such as the thyroid and adrenal glands, are called *endocrine* glands. (Endo means "inside.") Endocrine glands do not have ducts; they produce hormones that are carried by the bloodstream to the places in the body where they do their jobs. The pancreas is a kind of combination gland which produces both endocrine hormones such as insulin and digestive enzymes that are exocrine secretions. Endocrine glands are not directly affected by CF—not even the endocrine parts of the pancreas.

Mucus helps to protect the lungs and air passages by removing germs and dust. It coats other ducts and passageways in the body, too, acting as a lubricant to allow secretions and other body products to pass through more easily.

Normally mucus is thin and slippery, but when a person has CF, the mucus-producing cells absorb too much water. So the mucus becomes thick and sticky, and it can clog up ducts and passageways. When a mucous plug forms in the pancreas or liver, it blocks the flow of digestive enzymes to the intestine. Then the enzymes are not able to do their job, and food is not digested properly. In addition, the mucous plugs cause enzyme-producing cells to be destroyed and replaced by scar tissue, which makes even less enzymes available for digestion.

In males, mucous plugs stop up ducts leading out of the testes and prevent sperm from passing through. (These are the same ducts that are cut in a vasectomy, to make a man sterile.) As a result, most adult males with cystic fibrosis are unable to father children, although they can have a normal sex life.

The worst problem is thick mucus in the lungs. It accumulates and blocks breathing tubes, making breathing difficult. The thick mucous plugs also form an environment in which bacteria can grow easily. This causes frequent infections, which scar and weaken the lungs. The lungs become less able to work effectively as more tissue is

A diseased lung is the result of mucous plugs, which develop from an improperly functioning exocrine gland.

destroyed. Nearly all people with CF eventually develop this chronic lung disease, and lung damage is the most frequent cause of death among people with cystic fibrosis.[2]

SYMPTOMS OF CF

Most parents are quite surprised when their child is diagnosed with cystic fibrosis. Usually both parents are healthy, and often there are no known genetic diseases in their family history. Pregnancy and birth proceed normally. The child usually seems quite healthy and may have a healthy appetite. But he or she just doesn't seem to gain any weight, and seems to be getting colds constantly. Today most doctors suspect cystic fibrosis when they see this combination of problems.

But diagnosing cystic fibrosis is not always easy. All CF patients are born with the disease, but the severity and the timing of the first symptoms vary from person to person. In some children the lungs are most affected; other children have more digestive problems.

The early symptoms of cystic fibrosis are the same as those of many other health problems that children may suffer, such as asthma, or various digestive disorders. Or symptoms may be very mild during the early years. Some children do not develop any symptoms until they reach adolescence. For these reasons, some people with cystic fibrosis may go for many years without being diagnosed.

However, most often CF is diagnosed before a child is four years old. One out of ten cystic fibrosis patients is diagnosed at birth. Doctors know these babies have CF because they are born with an intestinal blockage called *meconium ileus*.

Some babies are diagnosed even before they develop symptoms after routine screenings are performed because someone else in the family had CF.

COMMON CYSTIC FIBROSIS SYMPTOMS* INCLUDE:[3]

1. salty-tasting skin
2. persistent coughing
3. large amounts of mucus
4. failure to gain weight
5. frequent, greasy, bulky, and foul-smelling bowel movements
6. persistent wheezing
7. recurring pneumonia
8. nasal polyps (small growths inside the nose)
9. enlargement of fingertips and toes ("clubbing")

* A person does not have to have all these symptoms to have CF. The symptoms vary from one person to another.

TESTING FOR CF

If a doctor suspects cystic fibrosis because of a child's symptoms, or if someone else in the family is known to have the disease, the child will be given a *sweat test*. This is one of the most important tests to confirm the possibility of CF. Sweat glands are exocrine glands and are affected by the disease. So a person who has CF will have normal amounts of sweat, but—because the faulty cells are absorbing too much water—the amount of salt (sodium and chloride) and potassium in the sweat is abnormally high.

The doctor places a pad or piece of filter paper on the child's forearm or back to absorb the sweat. Then the area is wrapped up in plastic. Using a harmless chemical called *pilocarpine* and small bursts of electricity, the sweat glands

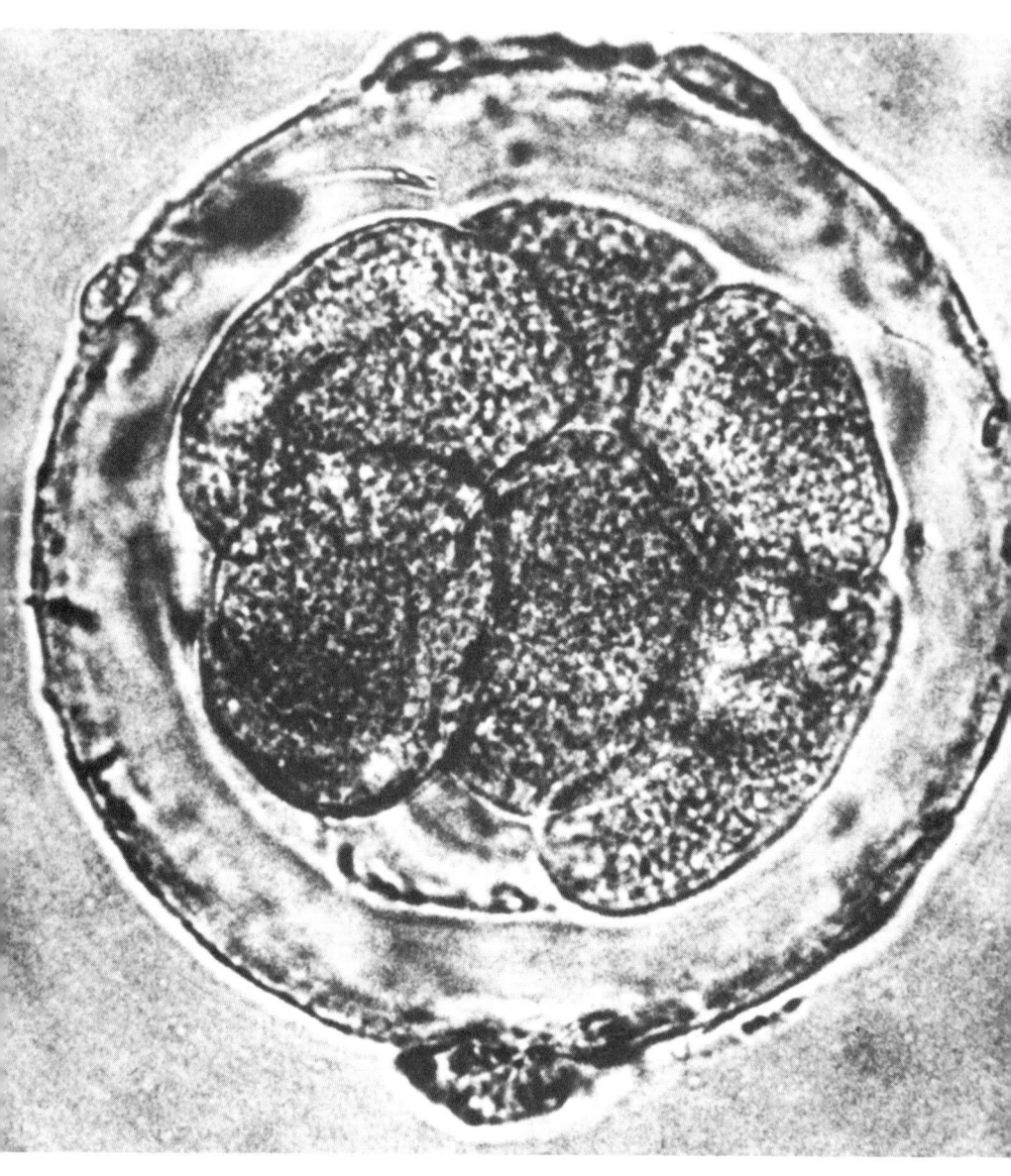

The growing human embryo. New methods are being developed to test embryos for cystic fibrosis.

are stimulated to produce more sweat. After a while the plastic is removed, and the pad is sent to the laboratory to be analyzed.

If the sweat test shows that the sweat contains too much salt, another sweat test will usually be conducted to make sure. This test is usually very accurate in determining whether or not a person has CF, but it cannot predict how severe the symptoms may become.

If a child is found to have CF, any brothers and sisters (and sometimes even cousins) are usually tested too.

A blood test called the *immunoreactive trypsinogen test* (*IRT*) can be used to test newborns.[4] In some newborn nurseries, a sample of blood is taken for this test two or three days after birth. A positive IRT is then double-checked with a sweat test.

Doctors can use genetic testing to find out if a baby has CF even before it is born, by removing some cells and examining the chromosomes. In one method, called *amniocentesis*, a small amount of fluid that surrounds the fetus is removed. This "amniotic fluid" is examined under a microscope and analyzed biochemically. A small piece of the placenta can also be removed and examined. (This method is called *chorionic villus biopsy*.)[5] Genetic testing methods are used when a couple has already had a child with CF, or if the disease has been found in a close relative.

In vitro fertilization clinics, which help parents who are unable to have children naturally, are developing ways to test embryos before they are implanted inside the mother to make sure that they will not have cystic fibrosis. Researchers have removed a cell from an embryo when it was only four cells big, and have checked the genes before the embryo was implanted in the mother. And at the Masonic Medical Center, researcher Yury Verlinsky even tested an unfertilized egg from a woman who was afraid she might have a child with CF. The tests showed no signs of CF, and the woman had a healthy baby.[6]

4
RESPIRATORY PROBLEMS

Almost everyone with CF will eventually suffer from lung disease. Respiratory problems are the most serious symptoms of cystic fibrosis. How well a person with CF can get along and how long he or she will live depend mainly on how serious the lung problems are.

"All of the treatments of cystic fibrosis take aim at the same deadly enemy—lung infections. That is why children die," wrote Jacquie Gordon in her book about her daughter Christine. "Christine and I hated the whole process . . . but we had no choice. 'Thumps' would keep her alive."[1] ("Thumps" refers to a type of physical therapy in which the patient's back is slapped very hard to loosen mucus in the lungs.) And in spite of her severe cystic fibrosis, Christine won a special award at her high-school graduation, danced at her senior prom, and even sang with a rock band.

OUR RESPIRATORY SYSTEM

The organs of the respiratory system are responsible for supplying oxygen to the body (Figure 1). Oxygen, which makes up about one-fifth of the gases in the air we

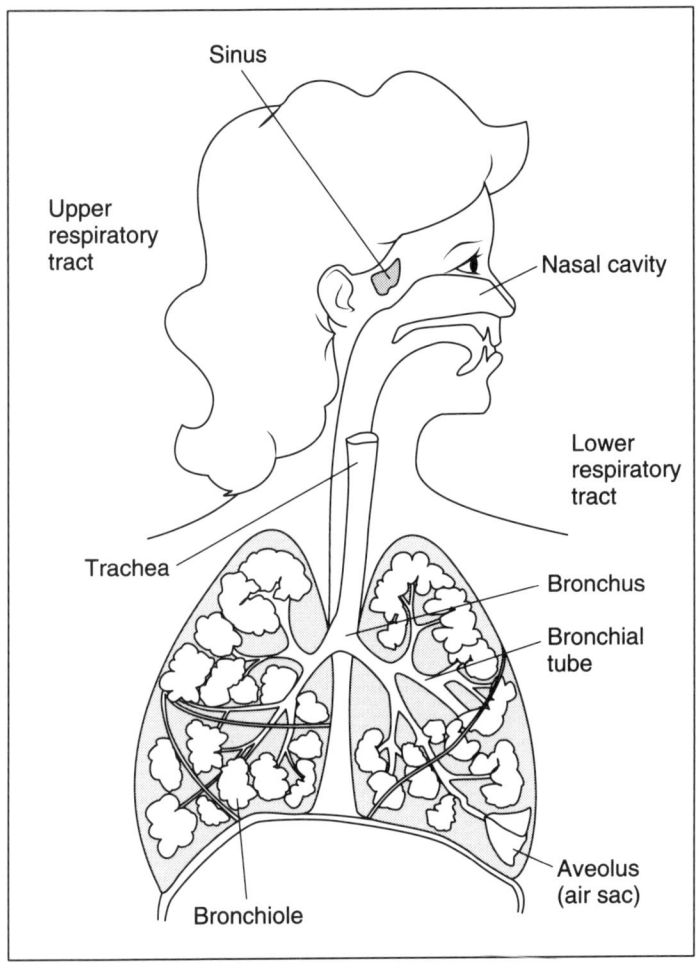

FIGURE 1. *The respiratory system*

breathe, is needed for energy inside each of our cells. The human respiratory system includes our two lungs and the tubes that carry air to them.

The respiratory system has two main parts. The *upper respiratory tract* includes the nose and sinuses. Air is breathed in through the nose and mouth. Dust and germs in the air are trapped in the sticky layer of mucus that coats the lining of the upper respiratory tract and filtered out of the air flow. The mucus-coated lining of the nose also helps to warm cold air and adds moisture to dry air.

The *lower respiratory tract* starts at the windpipe, or trachea. The trachea branches out into two large tubes, called *bronchi*. One bronchus enters the right lung, and one enters the left lung. Each bronchus branches into smaller and smaller tubes that spread throughout the lungs like the branches and twigs on a tree. The smallest branches are called *bronchioles*, which eventually end in tiny air sacs. Each air sac contains about twenty cup-shaped cavities, called *alveoli*.

There are millions of alveoli in each lung. In fact, if you could spread the walls of the alveoli out flat, they would take up half a tennis court or about fifty times the surface area of the skin that covers our bodies.[2] When we breathe in air, the air sacs inflate and deflate like very small balloons. Oxygen in the sacs passes into tiny blood capillaries in the walls of the alveoli. The capillaries carry the oxygen into larger blood vessels, which transport it around the body. Waste gases, such as carbon dioxide, are carried by the blood from body cells to the alveoli, then exhaled from the lungs.

Some particles make it past the upper respiratory tract's filtering system and end up in the lower respiratory tract. Dust or soot particles could block the tiny air tubes and prevent oxygen from being brought into the body, and waste products like carbon dioxide from being taken away. Bacteria or viruses could also cause an infection in the lungs.

But the airways in the lower respiratory tract, like the passages in the nose and throat, are coated with a thin, slippery layer of mucus. It keeps the airway lining from drying out and also traps dust and other particles.

Gravity would normally draw mucus and debris deep into the lungs because people spend a good deal of time in

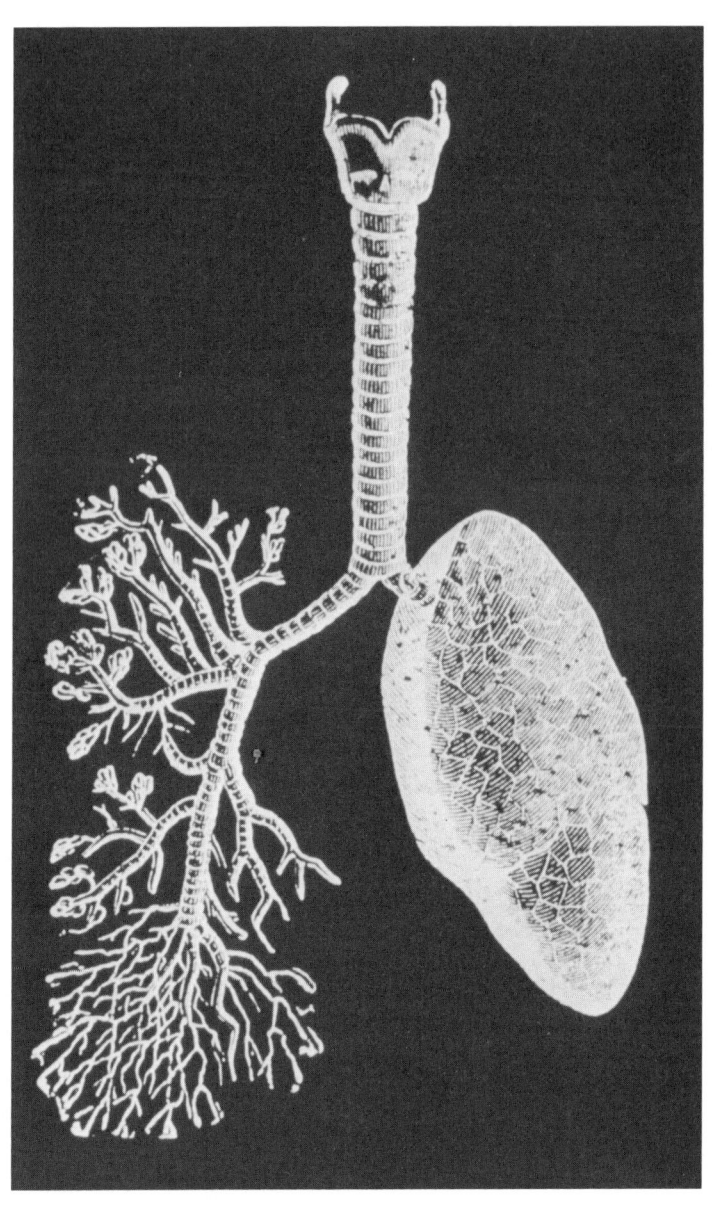

This illustration of the lungs shows a view of the inner bronchi on the left.

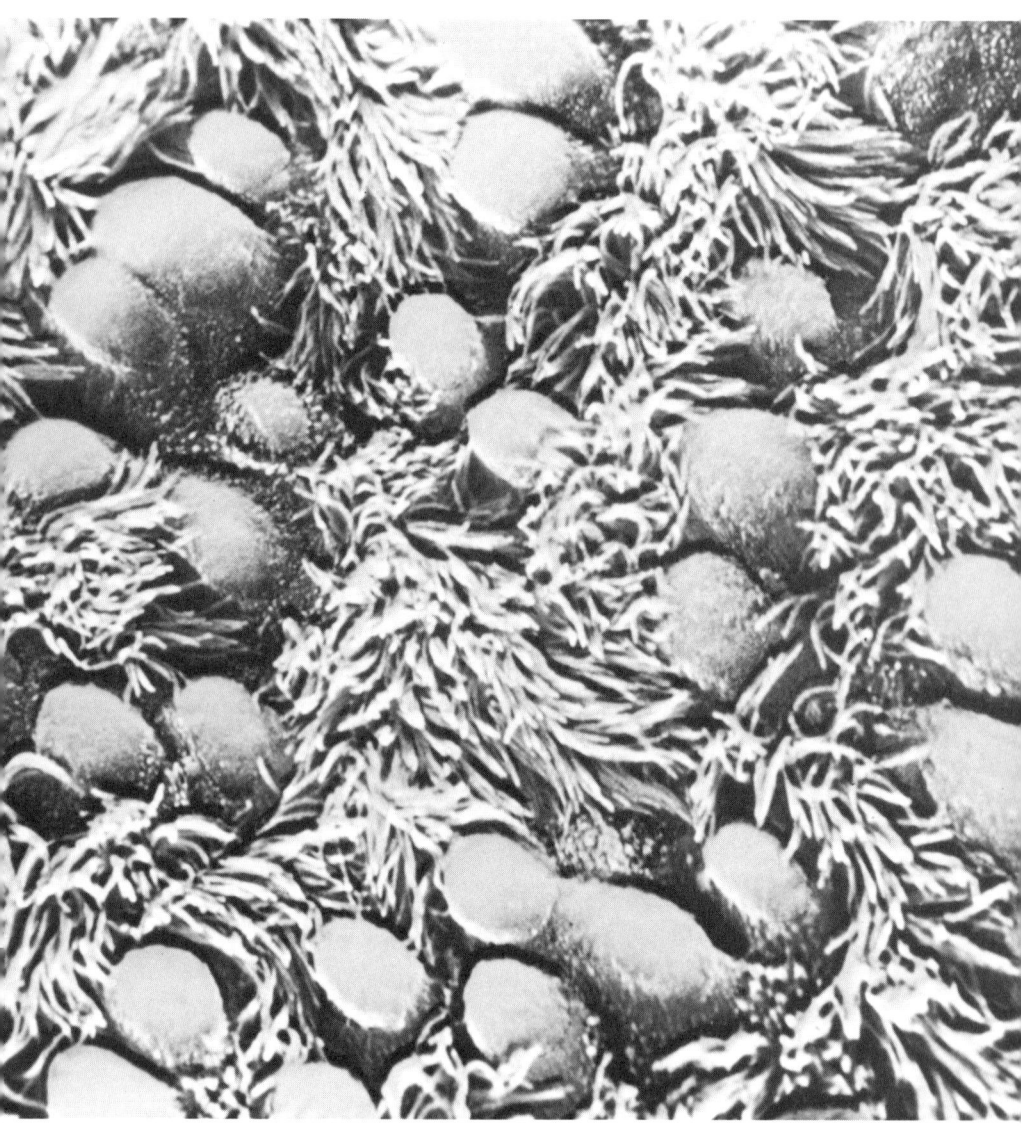

The interior lining of the lung contains clumps of fine hairlike cilia, which surround the round cells, whose function is to release mucus. In a cystic fibrosis sufferer too much mucous is released.

an upright position. But cells in the lining have special hair-like structures called *cilia*, which wave back and forth to create currents in the mucus. This action works against gravity to help sweep the trapped particles up toward the throat. They are removed from the airway when the mucus is coughed up or swallowed.

LOWER RESPIRATORY TRACT PROBLEMS

When a person has cystic fibrosis, the mucus becomes thick and sticky—so thick that the cilia cannot move it along properly (Figure 2). Mucus is supposed to help clear the breathing passages, but in CF the sticky mucus forms a mucous plug instead, and stops up small airways. Then air can't get into the alveolar sacs, and the exchange of oxygen for carbon dioxide cannot take place.

People with CF tend to cough frequently, trying to bring up the mucus that is clogging their breathing passages. (Young children often swallow their phlegm, so none is being coughed out, but that does not mean there is no mucus in their lungs.) As the mucus builds up, the natural clearing action of coughing becomes less effective.

The germs that the mucus was supposed to carry up to the throat to get rid of start to grow and multiply, which can lead to lung infections. That is why people with CF suffer from frequent lung infections.

Recurring lung infections can damage the cilia lining the airways, causing them to work even less effectively. Also, when an infection develops, the body produces more mucus. In a healthy person this is a protective reaction, which helps to flush out the harmful germs. But in someone with CF this only causes more mucous plugs and makes the situation even worse. A vicious circle develops, in which the mucous plugs cause lung infections, which cause more mucus to be produced, which causes even more mucous plugs to form, spreading the infection.

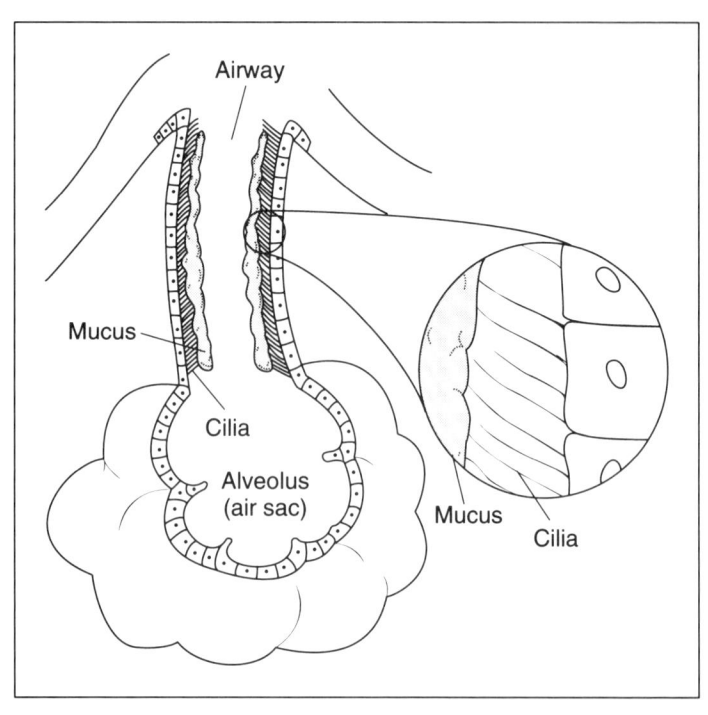
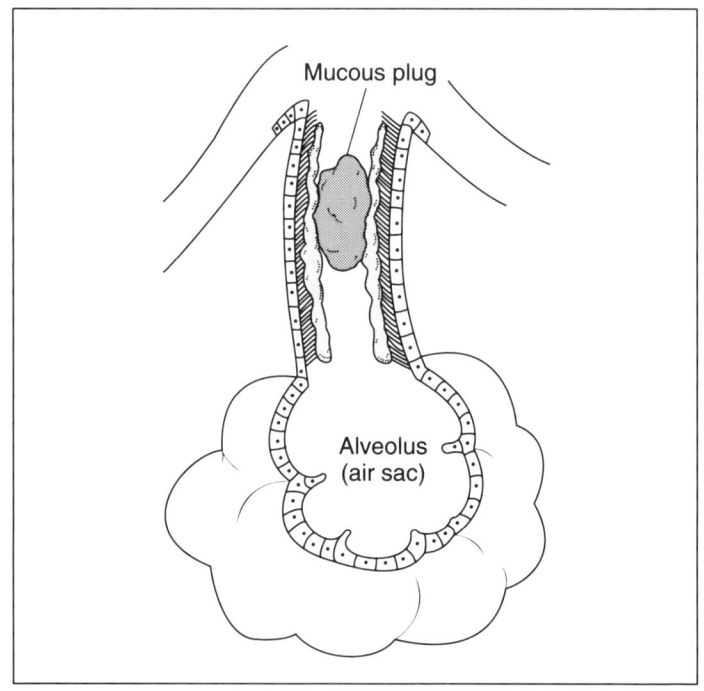

In the early stages of CF, *Staphylococcus aureus* bacteria, often called staph (pronounced "staff"), are the most common bacteria that cause lung infections. (In the general public this microorganism can cause anything from pimples to serious bone infections.)[3]

Later in the course of cystic fibrosis another bacterium, *Pseudomonas aeruginosa*, often called pseudomonas (pronounced "soo-doe-mow-nas"), becomes the most common infection-causing microorganism.[4] Pseudomonas does not normally attack healthy tissue. But the damaged tissue in the airways that is formed as CF progresses makes a prime target for this bacterium. Once pseudomonas is established in the lungs, it is very hard to get rid of.

UPPER RESPIRATORY TRACT PROBLEMS

CF may also affect the nose and sinuses (the upper respiratory tract). Most people with CF (more than 90 percent) suffer from sinusitis.[5] When the thick mucus blocks the sinuses, they can become infected and inflamed. Antihistamines and decongestants may help to reduce the inflammation, making it easier to breathe, and antibiotics help control infections.

FIGURE 2.
Cilia are hairlike structures on cells in the lungs that push mucus to the throat. In cystic fibrosis, mucous plugs keep air from getting into or out of the alveoli.

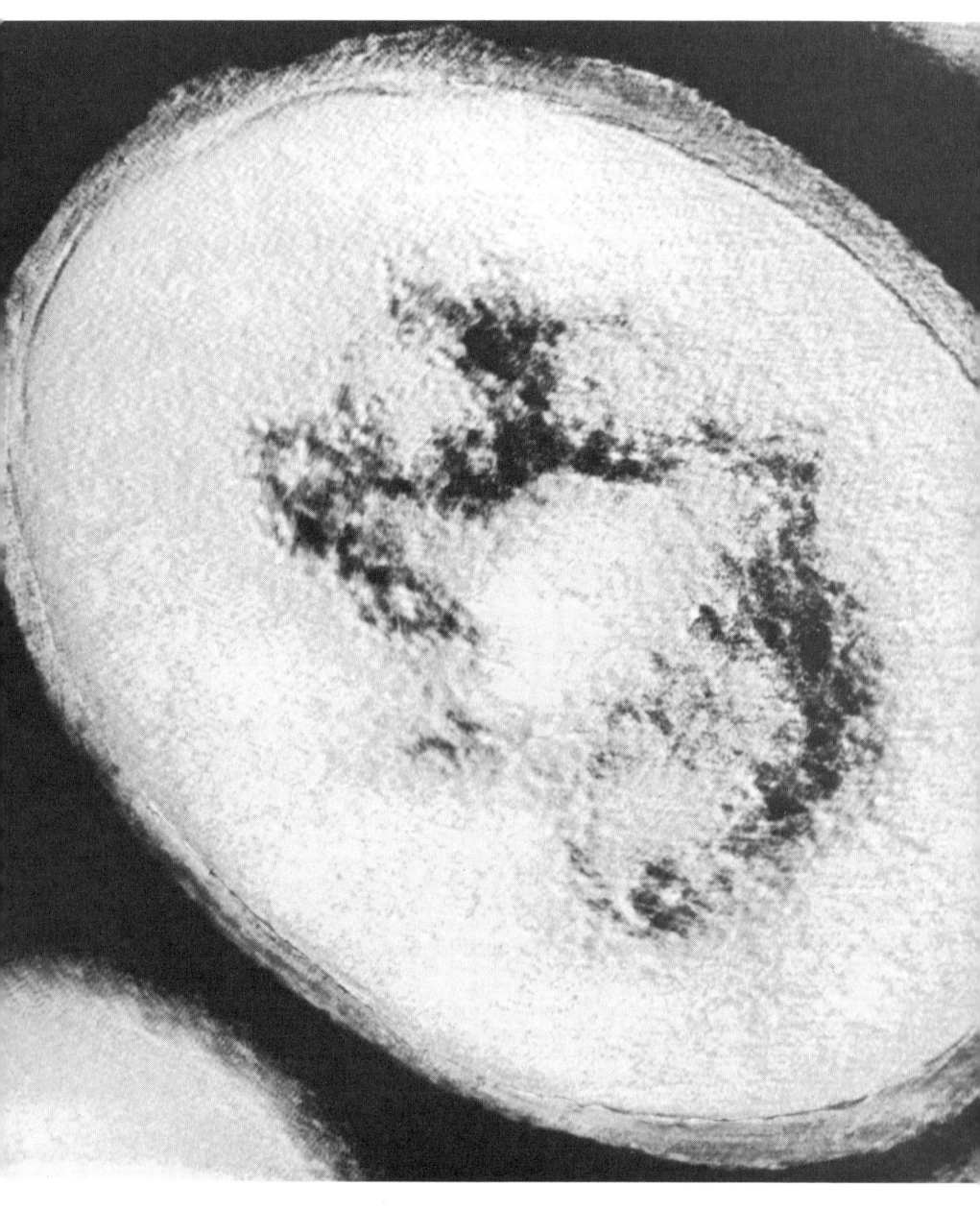

Very often, the Staphylococcus aureus *bacteria grow in the lungs of cystic fibrosis sufferers, causing infection.*

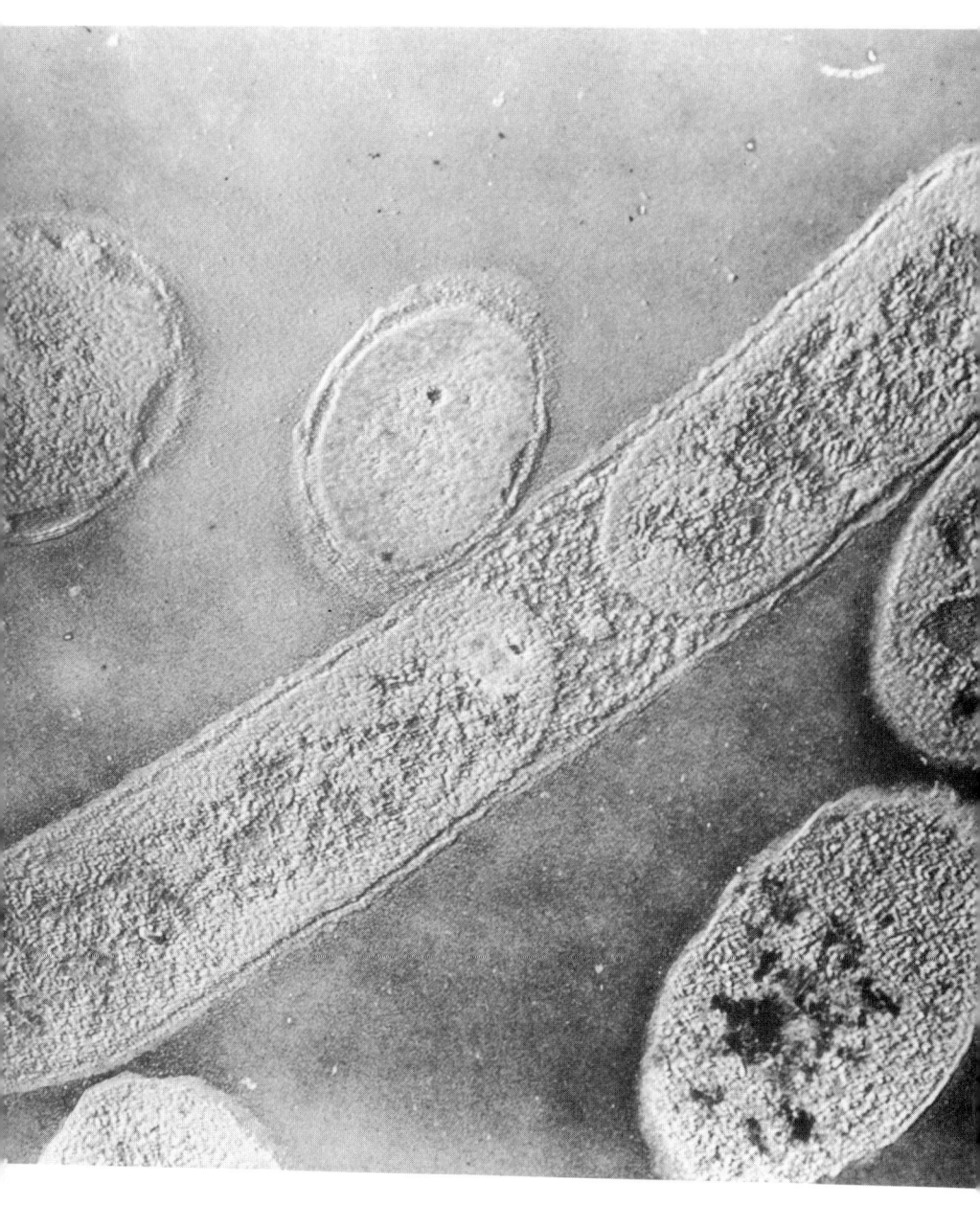

Pseudomonas aeruginosa *is another bacterium that attacks the lungs.*

About 15 percent of the people with CF also develop nasal polyps,[6] which are small growths inside the nose. If these polyps block the nasal passages, they may have to be surgically removed. But they often tend to grow back again.

OTHER COMPLICATIONS

Almost all people with CF eventually find that the tips of their fingers and toes become enlarged. This is called *clubbing*. It is not known exactly why clubbing occurs, but it also occurs with other lung diseases as well.

The walls of the airways of almost all patients with CF eventually become inflamed and damaged. The bronchi can eventually become weak and stretched out—a condition called *bronchiectasis*. This makes it even harder to clear mucus from the airways and can make breathing more difficult.

As the disease progresses, some patients develop a barrel-shaped chest. Air is trapped in the lungs because of mucous plugs, and the rib cage gradually becomes enlarged. This also occurs with other lung diseases.

In about one out of twenty-five CF patients,[7] the lung tissue or airways become so damaged that a part will rupture or tear. In this condition, called *pneumothorax*, air leaks out of the tear and can become trapped between the lung and the chest wall. In mild cases of pneumothorax the air goes back into the lungs by itself, or the patient may only need extra oxygen for a while. But as more air leaks out the lung may collapse, causing severe breathing problems. Some people may need to have the air drained, and others may need lung surgery.

It is not uncommon for people with CF to have blood streaks in the mucus that they cough up. The airway linings become damaged easily because of frequent infections, and the inflammation and irritation can cause a little

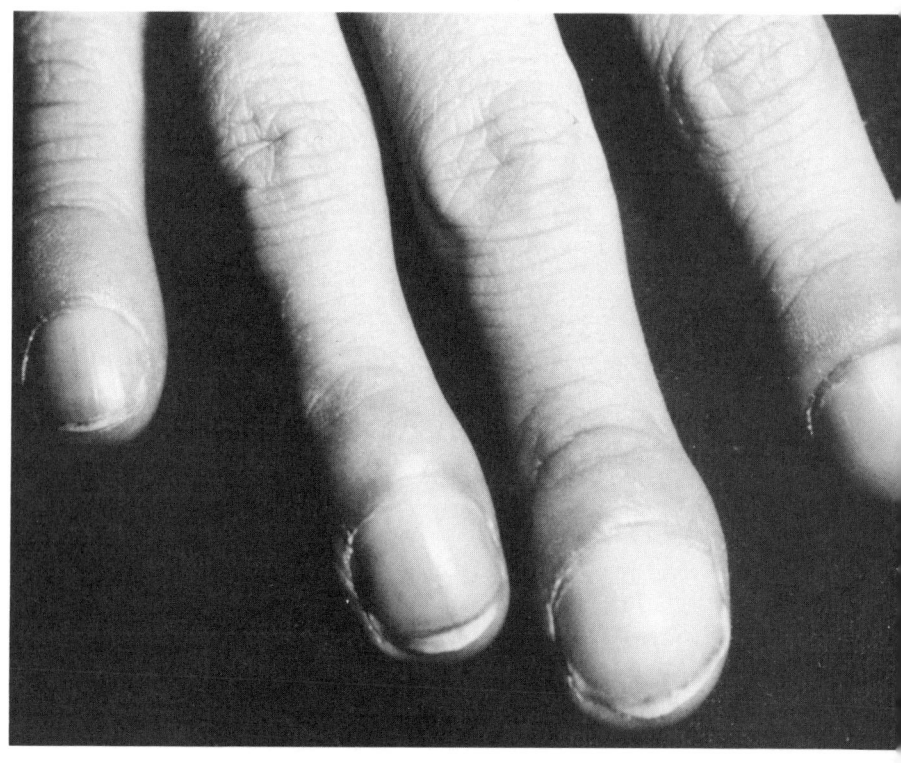

Clubbed fingers is often a symptom of cystic fibrosis.

bleeding. Coughing up blood, called *hemoptysis*, is usually not dangerous. Sometimes blood in the sputum is more serious, however, if the blood is from an artery that was damaged. Fortunately, this is rarely the case.

Over time the damage to the lungs causes the lungs to work much less efficiently, and not enough oxygen is delivered to the blood. To compensate, the heart has to work harder to pump more blood to the lungs. The blood pressure in the arteries that go from the heart to the lungs may also be increased, which makes the heart work even harder. This extra strain can cause the right side of the heart to become larger, which is called *cor pulmonale*. If the condition worsens, the heart may become unable to circulate blood properly.

DIAGNOSIS AND EVALUATION

Today most children who are diagnosed with CF are referred to a special cystic fibrosis clinic. The staff at these clinics is specially trained for cystic fibrosis care and treatment. Most patients make regular visits to the CF clinic.

The doctor will watch a child's progress carefully. He or she will be concerned with noting symptoms as well as how the child is feeling and acting. Certain tests will also help the doctor figure out what the disease is doing and what the best treatment plan might be.

Chest X rays are usually taken at least once a year to help the doctor see how the disease has affected the lungs. Breathing tests, or "pulmonary function tests," are done much more often to give an even better idea of how the lungs are functioning.

A healthy adult normally breathes in about a pint of air with every breath. As much as five times as much can be breathed in with a slow, deep breath. Doctors can gauge how well a CF patient's lungs are doing by checking how much air the lungs can move in and out. (This is called the *vital capacity*.) The person breathes in as deeply as possible and then breathes out slowly into a device called a spirometer, which measures the vital capacity. The doctor will keep a careful record of these measurements to compare how the lungs are functioning over a period of time. This helps to gauge how successful treatment has been. Pulmonary function tests are only performed on older children because they are hard to do with infants and young children.

A patient's sputum, or phlegm, is checked periodically to see if there is an infection in the lungs. Some mucus is

A young boy using a spirometer, a device that measures the vital capacity of the lungs

placed in a special dish that allows bacteria like staph and pseudomonas to grow and multiply. After a period of time the dish is checked to see if these bacteria are present. Blood tests are also done periodically.

SETTING UP A TREATMENT PLAN

For most people with CF, long-term pulmonary disease is the most serious problem. With proper treatment, though, the damage to the lungs can usually be slowed down. The doctor will set up a treatment program that will help to keep the airways from becoming blocked, as well as to prevent and treat lung infections.

CHEST PHYSICAL THERAPY

Chest physical therapy (CPT or chest physiotherapy) is designed to help prevent the airways from becoming blocked, by helping to move the mucus toward the throat.

The child sits or lies in a position that allows a part of the lung to drain toward the throat. (This is called *bronchial drainage*, BD, *or postural drainage, PD*.) The force of gravity helps pull the mucus through the small airways into larger ones and eventually to the throat, where it can be coughed up.

Meanwhile the area of the chest that is being drained is clapped, or *percussed* to help free up the mucus and get it moving. Then the patient sits up, coughs to bring up the mucus, and spits it out into a cup. The procedure is then repeated in different positions to help drain other parts of the lungs. About a dozen different positions are used to drain all the different areas of the lungs.

CPT is usually done one to three times a day, and each bronchial drainage treatment takes up to 30 minutes. It is usually done at home with a parent or other relative help-

Treatment for cystic fibrosis includes (a) antibiotics (b) chest physiotherapy, or "thumping"; and (c) inhalant treatments.

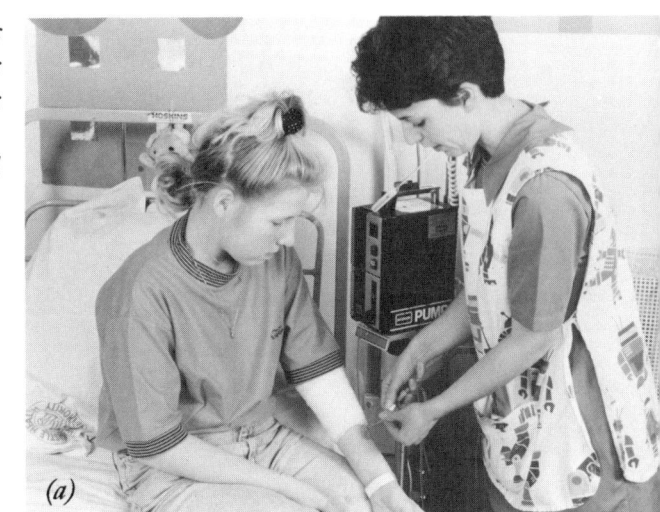

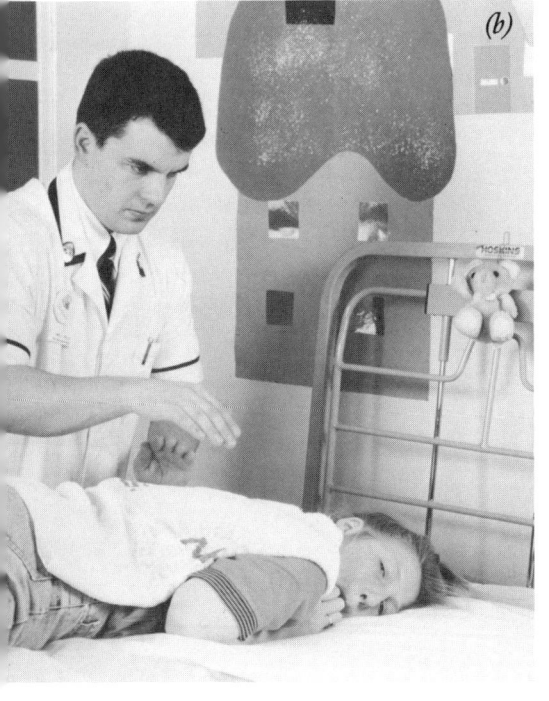

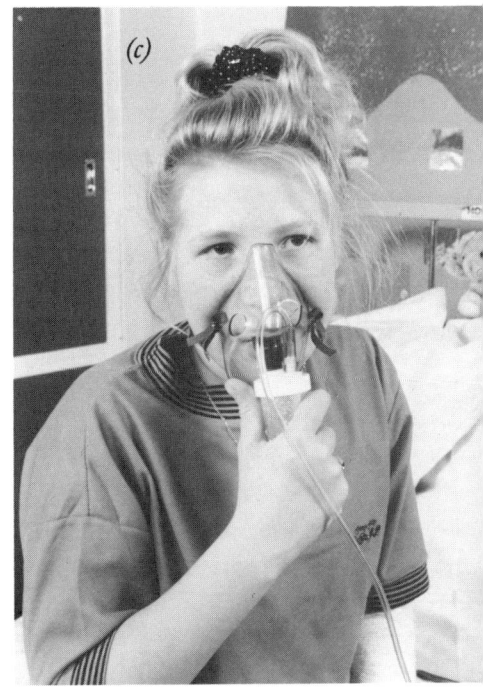

ing. Many patients can learn to perform their own chest physiotherapy. Mechanical devices such as electric chest clappers (mechanical percussors) and vibrators make this easier to accomplish. These devices are often very useful for adolescents and young adults who don't want to rely so much on parents and other caregivers.

The doctor will design a treatment plan which includes the specific positions, the amount of time spent in each position, and the number of times each day the therapy must be done.

MEDICATIONS

Several different types of medicines are used to treat the respiratory problems of cystic fibrosis. Rather than swallowing pills or liquids, many medications can be breathed right into the lungs in the form of an aerosol. A liquid medication is usually mixed with a saltwater (saline) solution and then turned into a mist that the person can inhale through a mask or a mouthpiece.

Decongestants help shrink swollen membranes that line the breathing tubes. *Bronchodilators* make breathing tubes wider, which makes it easier to breathe. *Mucolytics* make the mucus easier to drain by thinning it out. Some of these medications may be sprayed into the lungs before chest physical therapy, to make it more effective.

EXERCISE

Another important way of keeping the lungs clear is exercise. Most children with CF can take part in most physical activities such as sports and games, swimming and bicycling, and they are usually encouraged to do so. Exercise can be beneficial to people with CF for many reasons. Just as for children without CF, it helps build up strength in the heart and breathing muscles. Exercise also helps loosen up the mucus in the lungs and stimulates coughing, which helps clear the mucus out of the lungs. A Swedish study found that vigorous exercise was as effective as chest physiotherapy. The study also noted that the "psychological advantage was great and ... contributed to a more independent childhood and a better quality of life for these patients."[8] However, the condition of some CF children's lungs or heart may not allow them to participate in vigorous exercise. The doctor will advise whether an exercise program will be beneficial to a particular child. Children with CF also usually need to drink extra fluids and take extra salt when they exercise.

After adolescence, boys with CF often are healthier than girls with CF. One reason may be because boys usually have better developed chest muscles. Exercises like swimming help build up chest muscles and improve the ability of the lungs to function. Physiotherapy and exercise to train the chest muscles are important not just when the child has a cough but all the time, so the child will stay healthy.

ANTIBIOTIC TREATMENT

Antibiotics are used to help the body fight infections. These drugs are usually an important part of therapy because respiratory infections occur frequently in CF. Antibiotics kill the bacteria that cause infections. Some people need to take antibiotics all the time; others need them only once in a while—it all depends on the person and how the disease has affected the body. Antibiotics have greatly helped to extend the lifespan and quality of life for people with CF.

Antibiotics can be taken by three different methods. They can be swallowed in tablets or capsules (*oral antibiotics*), they can be given in a liquid form directly into the

Exercise not only clears the lungs, but is good for the mental well-being of cystic fibrosis sufferers. The two boys in the middle suffer from cystic fibrosis, but are preparing for the New York Marathon.

blood (*intravenous or IV antibiotics*), or they can be inhaled in a mist (*aerosolized antibiotics*).

Mild flare-ups are often treated with oral antibiotics. When lung infections are more serious, IV antibiotics may be given. The patient may have to stay in the hospital for IV treatment, or may be able to receive treatment at home.

Aerosol antibiotics go right into the airways, rather than having to pass through the digestive system and into the blood before finally reaching the lungs. Some antibiotics are effective when taken this way. Aerosol antibiotics are sometimes taken after chest physical therapy. Mucus has been removed from the lungs, and the antibiotic can work better.

People with CF usually take antibiotics over long periods of time. But a particular antibiotic may gradually become less effective because bacteria may develop resistance to it. For this reason, a doctor may change the type of antibiotic after a while, or combine the treatment with other antibiotics.

Some childhood illnesses can affect the lungs, so it is important for children with CF to receive all the normal immunization shots, as well as a flu shot each year. Some parents whose children have CF may try to overprotect their children and keep them inside so that they will not catch any sicknesses from other children. But it is impossible to protect children from all germs, and a child's emotional and mental health and growth depend on living as normal a life as possible. The doctor may simply advise that the child should avoid unnecessary contact with anyone who has a cold or other contagious illness—the same advice that would be good for any child.

Sometimes children with CF will try not to cough because they are embarrassed about coughing all the time. But that can be harmful. Coughing is very important because it helps to loosen and remove mucus from the air passages. Friends sometimes think that they can catch CF when a person with CF coughs, but of course, you can't "catch" CF because this disease is not caused by germs. Either people are born with it or they aren't.

Cough suppressants are not good for children with CF. These medicines relieve symptoms, but they do not remove mucus from the lungs. If the child coughs more than usual, this may be a sign that there is a lung infection that should be treated. Mist tents and oral expectorants (medications that supposedly help loosen up mucus) are forms of treatment that are no longer commonly used. And doctors have not found any particular climate to be better for people with CF.[9]

5
DIGESTIVE PROBLEMS

When Steve was a baby he had a good appetite, but no matter how much he ate he gained hardly any weight at all. Finally, when he was one year old, doctors diagnosed cystic fibrosis and prescribed a supplement of digestive enzyme tablets. Taking these enzymes, Steve quickly put on weight and became a sturdy little boy. For a long time, there were no other signs of CF—he even competed on his high school's cross-country team. Lung problems did not develop until he was in his twenties. Now working as a science writer, Steve keeps up on all the latest medical facts—and still takes his digestive enzyme supplements.[1]

Our bodies need food to grow and function every day. More than forty different nutrients are needed for good health. Most foods contain some nutrients, but no single food contains all the nutrients we need. A varied diet of foods from all the major food groups (fruits; vegetables; cereals and breads; milk and dairy products; and meat, fish, nuts, and beans) usually supplies all of the nutrients that we need.

But the nutrients in foods are not usually in a form that the body can use. Most need to be broken down into smaller units first. This is done by the digestive system.

About 90 percent of people with cystic fibrosis have problems in digesting foods.[2] The severity of symptoms varies greatly with each individual, but with proper eating and digestive supplements the digestive problems of most CF patients can usually be kept under control.

HOW DOES THE DIGESTIVE SYSTEM WORK?

The process of digestion starts in the mouth when we chew our food. Chewing breaks the food down into smaller pieces, and enzymes in saliva start to break down some of the nutrients into smaller units. The food passes down the esophagus into the stomach, where powerful enzymes break down more of the complex nutrients. In the small intestine food is broken down further, and it is here that most nutrients are absorbed into the body (see Figure 3).

Exocrine glands in the *pancreas* make enzymes to help break down fats, starches, and proteins in the foods we eat. These digestive enzymes travel through small tubes called pancreatic ducts from the pancreas into the small intestine, where they can turn the complicated protein, starch, and fat molecules into simpler parts that the body can use.

The parts of food that are not used are excreted from the body. In the intestines mucus is produced by other exocrine glands so that waste products that are left over can leave the body more easily.

In most people with CF the secretions produced by the pancreas are too thick, and the digestive enzymes get stuck in the pancreatic ducts. Without these enzymes, the food can't be digested properly in the small intestine. So a lot of the protein and fat in the food can't be absorbed and used by the body. Failure of the body to absorb food properly is called *malabsorption*.

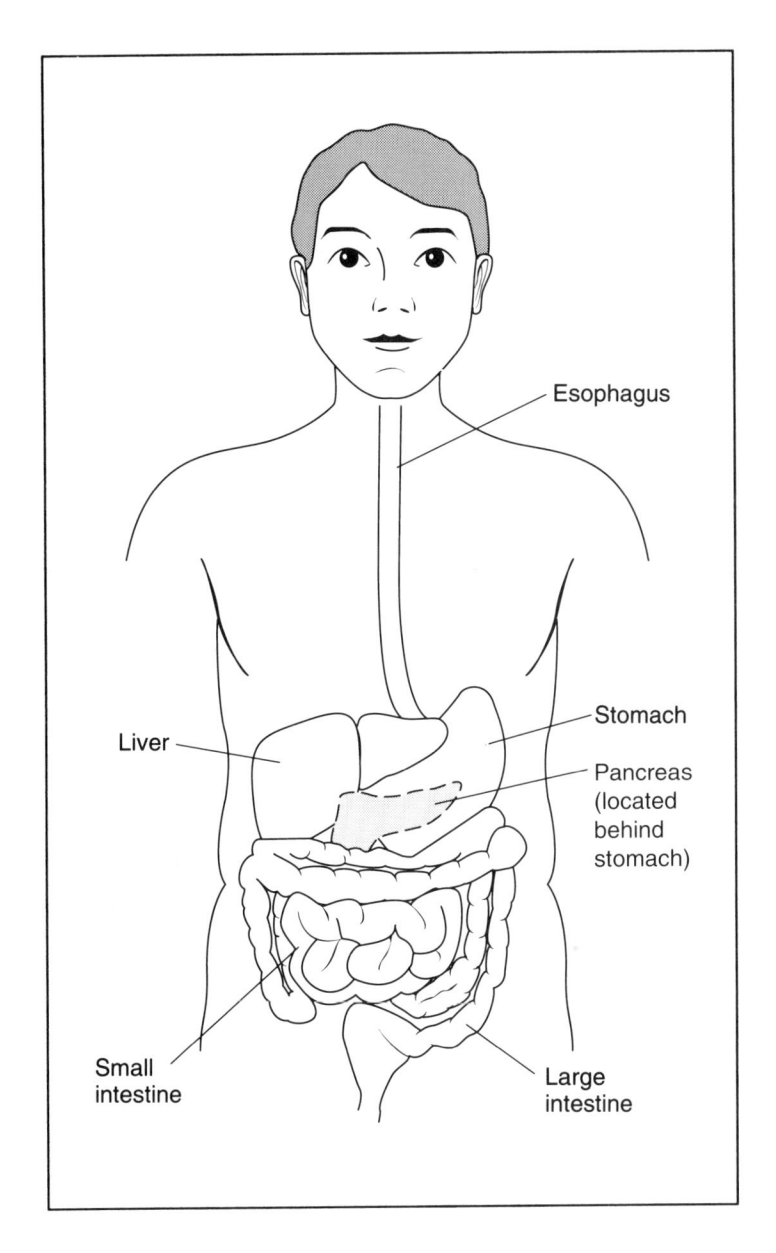

FIGURE 3. *The gastrointestinal system*

Proteins are very important for all people, but especially for children. They are needed to help us grow and to repair body tissues. Fats provide energy and also help the body to absorb vitamins. When these important nutrients are not absorbed properly, malnutrition can result. A person may be unable to gain weight, no matter how much food he or she eats, and muscle and fat tissue may decrease. A child's growth may slow down.

Lung disease also makes gaining weight even harder, because the body has to use up more calories than usual to breathe. Extra calories are also used in trying to repair the damage in the lungs. Without proper nutrients it is more difficult for the body to fight off lung infections, so a CF patient's overall health will also be much worse.

Another major symptom of digestive problems in cystic fibrosis is frequent, greasy, large, smelly bowel movements, which are produced because there is a lot of undigested fat. These irregular stools may also cause irritation or swelling in the bowel, which is why some children with CF often complain about pain or discomfort in the abdomen. Fat malabsorption causes cramps, gas, and flatus, too, and a CF patient's abdomen may bulge.

TESTING FOR DIGESTIVE PROBLEMS

Doctors know a baby with CF is having digestive problems when he or she is very slow in gaining weight. (In fact, "failure to thrive" even though the baby may have a good appetite can be one of the early signs pointing to CF.) For older patients, many different tests are available to determine how severe the digestive problems are. A stool sample may be stained with a dye that tests for fat. If the stain is very bright, doctors know there is a lot of fat in the feces, which means not much is being used by the body. The stool sample may also be tested for low levels of pancreatic enzymes.

TREATMENT OF DIGESTIVE PROBLEMS

There are three major types of treatments for digestive problems of CF. These include: (1) diet and nutrition; (2) pancreatic enzymes; and (3) vitamins.

Good nutrition is needed for all children to help them grow and develop properly, as well as to heal damaged tissues and cells, and for muscle strength and endurance. Eating a balanced diet provides most children with the nutrients they need to stay healthy. But just eating good foods may not be enough for children with CF, because not all of the nutrients are absorbed properly, and extra nutrients may be needed for keeping the lungs healthy. People with CF are usually advised to eat much more than the normal daily recommended allowance for people in their age group—sometimes as much as twice the calories![3] More frequent snacks and extra helpings at meals will usually make up this difference in calories.

Most Americans eat too much fat, and health experts advise cutting down on the amount of fat we eat. In the past, doctors recommended that children with cystic fibrosis eat less fat too, because malabsorption of fat causes digestive problems. But today, enzyme supplements are much better than they used to be, and experts recommend that children with CF eat at least a normal amount of fat.

Why more fat? Extra calories are important for most people with CF, and fat contains more than twice the calories of proteins and carbohydrates. And the body uses less oxygen to break down fat into energy than it does to break down carbohydrates or proteins for energy. This puts less strain on the lungs.

ENZYME SUPPLEMENTS

Cystic fibrosis patients may be prescribed specially prepared food that doesn't require pancreas juices for digestion. Or they may be given the missing pancreatic enzymes separately.

Most CF patients must take supplements of pancreatic enzymes with every meal and snack. These supplements replace the pancreatic enzymes that are being blocked on their way from the pancreas to the intestines. The enzymes are swallowed in tablet, powder, or capsule form, between half an hour before and half an hour after every meal and snack.[4]

The enzymes pass through the stomach and into the small intestine, where they help break down fats and proteins so these nutrients can be used by the body. A combination of enzyme supplements and proper nutrition has helped many children with cystic fibrosis to sustain nearly normal growth and development.

VITAMIN SUPPLEMENTS

Most children with CF take two multivitamin supplements each day to prevent vitamin deficiencies.[5] Vitamins A, D, E, and K are absorbed into the body with fats, and these fat-soluble vitamins may not be absorbed well in cystic fibrosis patients. Water-soluble forms of vitamins are better than fat-soluble ones for children with CF. Other vitamin supplements may be given, but parents are urged to give their children only the vitamins recommended by their physician. Some parents might think that if some vitamins are good, a lot are better. But some types of vitamins can be harmful, or even fatal if taken in large doses.

Some CF patients cannot get enough nutrients from their diets, even with enzyme and vitamin supplements. In addition to regular food intake, they may need to have tube feeding, in which a liquid supplement is fed directly into the stomach through a tube that passes through the nose. Others may receive nutrients intravenously, that is, in a liquid flowing directly into the bloodstream.

A child with cystic fibrosis being counseled on the use of pancreatic enzyme pills. Many cystic fibrosis sufferers require these supplements.

OTHER DIGESTIVE-SYSTEM COMPLICATIONS

Cystic fibrosis can also cause other complications, which may require more serious medical attention. One out of every ten people with CF is born with an intestinal blockage called *meconium ileus*.[6] Meconium is the waste material that is present in the intestinal tract of a fetus. Normally a baby will pass this mixture of intestinal secretions within a few hours after birth. But when the secretions are too thick, they can block the intestines. (The ileum is the lower part of the small intestine where the blockage occurs; hence the name *meconium ileus*.) This blockage may have to be removed using special enemas or with surgery.

Sometimes older patients develop an obstruction in the bowel, too, because of thick mucous secretions in the digestive tract, or because food is not digested properly. This condition, too, may require medical attention. The patient may need mucolytic agents (which help to break up the thick mucus and wastes in the intestine), enemas, or diet and enzyme supplements. In extreme cases, surgery may be necessary.

Abnormal stools that are difficult to pass, combined with excessive coughing and poor weight gain, can sometimes result in *rectal prolapse*, in which the inner lining of the rectum sticks out of the anus. This condition is usually corrected when pancreatic enzymes are taken with the diet, and it rarely occurs in patients who are more than five years old.

One out of twenty-five patients with CF may develop sugar diabetes (*diabetes mellitus*).[7] Diabetes mellitus is a condition in which sugar is not handled properly by the body. Too much sugar is present in the blood and urine. Insulin, which is produced by the endocrine portion of the pancreas, is supposed to keep the amount of sugar in the blood at a normal level. But it is believed that the scarring that occurs in the pancreas with CF may make it harder for insulin to get into the blood vessels. (In this case CF causes an endocrine problem indirectly.)

In a less severe condition, called *glucose intolerance*, the blood sugar level is less than what would be considered diabetic, but higher than normal. This condition is even more common, especially in older CF patients. About 40 percent of CF patients develop diabetes mellitus or glucose intolerance.[8]

One out of eight to ten people with CF develops gallstones because of the body's inability to handle fats and bile acids properly.[9] One out of twenty CF patients suffers from liver problems.[10] Ducts in the liver that drain bile can become clogged when the secretions become too thick. A type of *cirrhosis* (fibrous scarring) of the liver results.

6
OTHER BODY SYSTEMS

Cystic fibrosis has major effects on the respiratory and digestive systems. But it also directly affects other parts of the body and indirectly affects nearly every part of the body.

SWEAT GLANDS

The symptoms of respiratory and digestive problems may vary among patients with cystic fibrosis. But all CF patients have too much salt in their sweat.

Unlike the lungs and the pancreas, sweat glands are not physically damaged by the disease. Sweat does not become thick and sticky like mucus in patients with CF. Nor do CF patients have more sweat than normal. But the amount of salt in the sweat is two to five times the normal amount. Parents and grandparents sometimes first detect this telltale sign when they kiss a child and notice a salty taste.

Sweat's major function is to regulate the temperature of the body. When the body gets too hot, we sweat more. Heat is carried away as sweat evaporates on the skin's surface. We sweat all the time, even in the winter. (People normally produce from two to twelve cups of sweat a day!) Sweat also carries away some of the body's waste products.

Normally sodium and chloride are absorbed back into the body while the sweat is on its way to the skin's surface. (These minerals are needed to help transport water to the surface, but once it is there, the salt is reabsorbed to be used again.) In cystic fibrosis, however, the sweat glands cannot reabsorb salt back into the body properly.

There is no relationship between the amount of extra salt in the sweat and how severe other symptoms of CF will be, but the extra salt is the surest way of confirming the disease.

Loss of too much salt can be a problem in hot weather, during very strenuous exercise, or when a child has a fever. Salt depletion can cause fatigue, weakness, fever, muscle cramps, abdominal pain, vomiting, dehydration, and heat stroke.

Children with CF are sometimes given their own saltshaker so that they can get extra salt. They may even be encouraged to eat salty foods whenever possible. When they sweat more than normal, they need to remember to drink more fluids, too, so that they will not become dehydrated. (Some CF children must limit their salt intake for other medical reasons.)

REPRODUCTIVE SYSTEM

About 98 percent of males with CF are sterile.[1] Sperm are not able to travel from the testes because a mucous plug blocks the vas deferens or other tubes in the male reproductive system (Figure 4). In some cases this blockage occurs before a child is even born.

Sexual development and growth are not affected by CF directly because CF does not affect the sex hormones and glands. But sexual development may be slower because of nutritional problems.

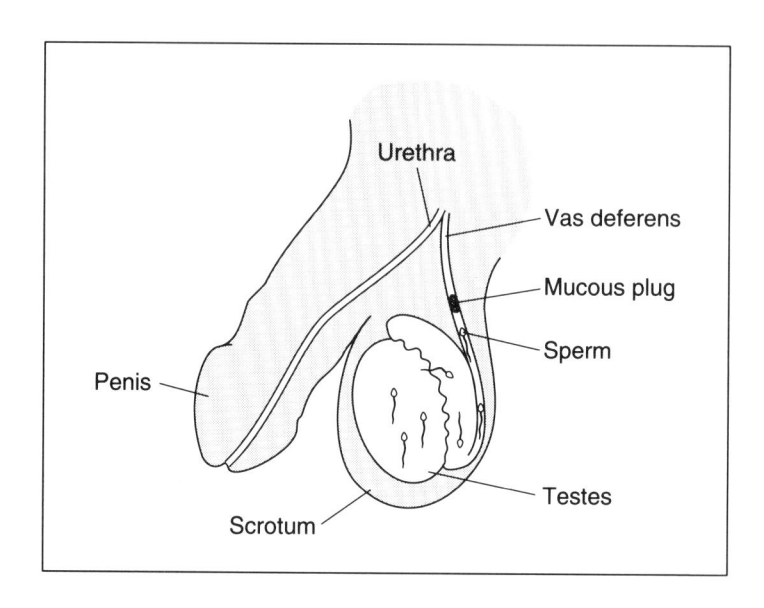

FIGURE 4. *Thick mucus secretions may block the vas deferens, the tube through which sperm travels from the testes to the prostate gland.*

Women with cystic fibrosis may have irregular menstrual cycles, and they may ovulate less often. Exocrine glands in the vagina secrete mucus to lubricate the vagina and provide fluid through which the sperm swim toward the uterus (Figure 5). But thick mucus in the vagina and the cervix can make it harder for sperm to get through to fertilize the egg. Women with CF may find it harder to become pregnant, although many do have successful pregnancies. How well the mother and fetus do is often related to how healthy the mother is during the pregnancy.

Women with cystic fibrosis are sometimes urged not to become pregnant because the strain on their bodies could worsen the condition of their lungs and heart. They are also sometimes cautioned about oral contraceptives,

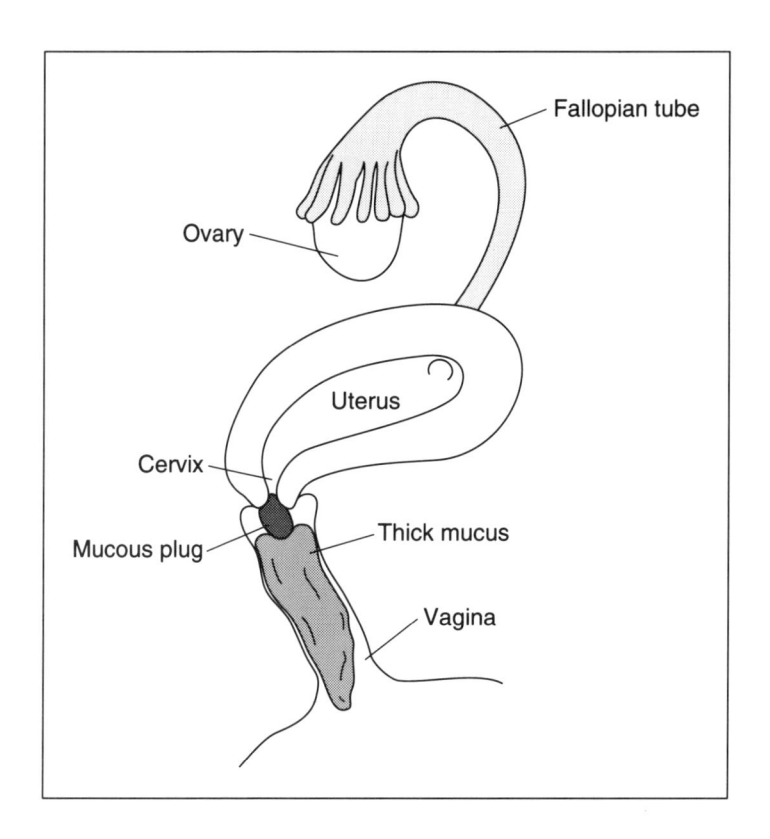

FIGURE 5. *Vaginal and cervical mucus may be so thick and sticky that sperm cannot move through it.*

which may make mucus even thicker. In women with CF this form of birth control may also increase the symptoms of liver disease or diabetes.

OTHER EFFECTS

The lung problems that are a major part of cystic fibrosis affect a child's growth and development. Children with

CF are often shorter than normal, or take longer to catch up in size to other children their age. Many children and young adults with cystic fibrosis feel pain in their ankles, knees, and wrists. Doctors are not yet exactly sure why, but they believe it has something to do with the lung disease. One in four CF patients develops an abnormal curvature of the spine called *kyphosis*.[2] This is the characteristic barrel-shaped chest caused by the enlarged lung volume in some CF patients.

7
A HEREDITARY DISEASE

Jimmy "The Greek" Snyder became famous for his calculations of the odds of various sports events. But odds also played an important role in his private life. He and his wife, Joan, had planned to have a large family. But their first daughter died three weeks after she was born. The doctors did not tell the grieving couple what was wrong with their baby. Two years later they had a healthy son. But little Jamie got sick a little while after his first birthday, and he never seemed to get well. He coughed all the time, and had diarrhea that wouldn't stop, and he was losing weight. Finally a doctor at a children's clinic gave the Snyders the diagnosis. "He has cystic fibrosis. I hope you're not ever going to have any more children," the doctor added. But Joan Snyder was already pregnant.

Their daughter Stephanie showed no signs of CF, and Jamie did well on a combination of percussion therapy and enzyme supplements. At the time, doctors knew CF was hereditary but were not sure exactly how it was inherited. So not even Jimmy "The Greek" could predict the odds for their next child. They had two more children: a healthy boy, and then a girl who died of CF at the age of two and a half.[1]

Jimmy the Greek, famous for calculating the odds of sports events, had several children born with cystic fibrosis, although neither he nor his wife have the disease.

GENETIC PLANS

Cystic fibrosis is a hereditary disease—the result of a mistake in one of our genes. Genes are the "genetic blueprints," or plans, for our bodies. When an embryo is developing inside its mother, each body part forms according to the detailed instructions spelled out in its genes. Genes are responsible for the color of our eyes and our hair and the shape of our nose. They help to determine whether we will be tall or short, and they tell the body which proteins and chemicals to manufacture to keep things going smoothly.

Just what are genes? They are parts of thread-like structures called *chromosomes*, which are found in a structure called the nucleus. (Most cells in the body have a nucleus, which is like the "brains" of the cell.) A chromosome contains many different genes. Each human cell contains a total of forty-six chromosomes, which can be matched up into twenty-three pairs.

Chromosomes are made up of DNA and protein. DNA is the chemical that contains the hereditary information that is passed from parents to their children. The DNA in a chromosome is a long chain formed from millions of smaller building blocks, called nucleotides or base pairs. Each gene carries the instructions for making a protein. The instructions are spelled out in a kind of code, which the body can translate from the DNA nucleotides into the amino acids that form the building blocks of proteins.

Scientists hope to someday map out all of the genes on the human chromosomes (which together are called the human genome), but this is no easy task. There are three billion base pairs in each set of forty-six chromosomes.[2]

A genetic disease occurs when something is wrong with a gene, which causes it to give the wrong instructions. Radiations, chemicals, and other things can produce changes, or *mutations*, in the DNA of the genes. Base pairs may be knocked out, or replaced by different ones, for example. Such changes in the genes may result in changes in the proteins they produce. In some genetic diseases a large portion of the gene may be damaged or missing. But in the case of cystic fibrosis, researchers have discovered that only a few of the tiny base pairs are missing—just three out of a total of about 250,000 base pairs in the whole gene (corresponding to just one amino acid in the protein it spells out) are enough to cause the disease.[3] Most people who have CF are missing the same amino acid in the same place on the protein produced by the gene. But other mutations are also possible. Scientists haven't even identified all the different mutations.

PLANS GONE WRONG

Every cell in our body contains the same full set of genetic blueprints. But not all of the genes are "turned on" in every cell. The cystic fibrosis gene, for example, is turned on only in *epithelial* cells. These are the cells that line the insides of tissues like the lungs, intestine, pancreas, and sweat glands in the skin.

The CF gene gives cells instructions to make a protein that is supposed to help epithelial cells (such as those that line the lungs) control the amount of water in the cells. But the instructions in the defective cystic fibrosis gene create a defective protein that causes epithelial cells to become mixed up. The cells absorb too much water. This takes water away from the mucus that coats the lining of the lungs, drying it out and making the mucus thick and sticky.

PATTERNS OF HEREDITY

Genes generally occur in pairs. In each pair of genes, one came from the mother and one from the father. This is how family traits are passed from parents to their children.

Some genes are *dominant* and some are *recessive*. If a dominant gene is present, the person will have that characteristic. But a characteristic determined by a recessive gene will show up only if the person has inherited two copies of this recessive gene, one from the mother and one from the father. For example if brown eyes is dominant and blue is recessive, a child will have blue eyes only if he or she receives a blue gene from the mother and a blue gene from the father. If the child's father contributed a brown gene and the mother a blue one, or if the child received a blue gene from the father and a brown one from the mother, the child will have brown eyes. A child who received a brown eye gene from each parent will have brown eyes, too; and there is no way to tell just by looking whether a brown-eyed child is carrying a recessive blue eye gene. (The actual inheritance of eye color is a bit more complicated than this simplified version; but this trait, like many others, is determined by combinations of dominant and recessive genes.)

The cystic fibrosis gene is a recessive gene. A person who has one cystic fibrosis gene and one normal gene will not have cystic fibrosis, because the normal gene is dominant. A child must receive the CF gene from both the mother *and* the father in order to have cystic fibrosis. Thus, a child can "inherit" cystic fibrosis from his or her parents even if neither of them has the disease.

A person with one cystic fibrosis gene is referred to as a *carrier* of the disease. If the father and the mother are both carriers, a child will inherit cystic fibrosis if a sperm with a cystic fibrosis gene unites with an egg with a cystic fibrosis gene. But as we'll see, that may not happen.

The cystic fibrosis gene is fairly common—nearly one out of twenty Americans is a carrier, and about one in every four hundred marriages is between cystic fibrosis carriers.

If both parents are carriers, half of the mother's eggs

and half of the father's sperm carry the CF gene. It is pure chance which sperm will unite with an egg, so there is no way to know or control which genes a parent passes to his or her children.

So these are the odds: When two carriers have a baby, there is a one in four chance (25 percent) that the baby will be born with CF. There is a 50 percent chance that the baby will be a carrier, and a 25 percent chance that the baby will not be a carrier.

If one parent has CF, will the children have CF too (Figures 6 and 7)? If the other parent is not a carrier, then

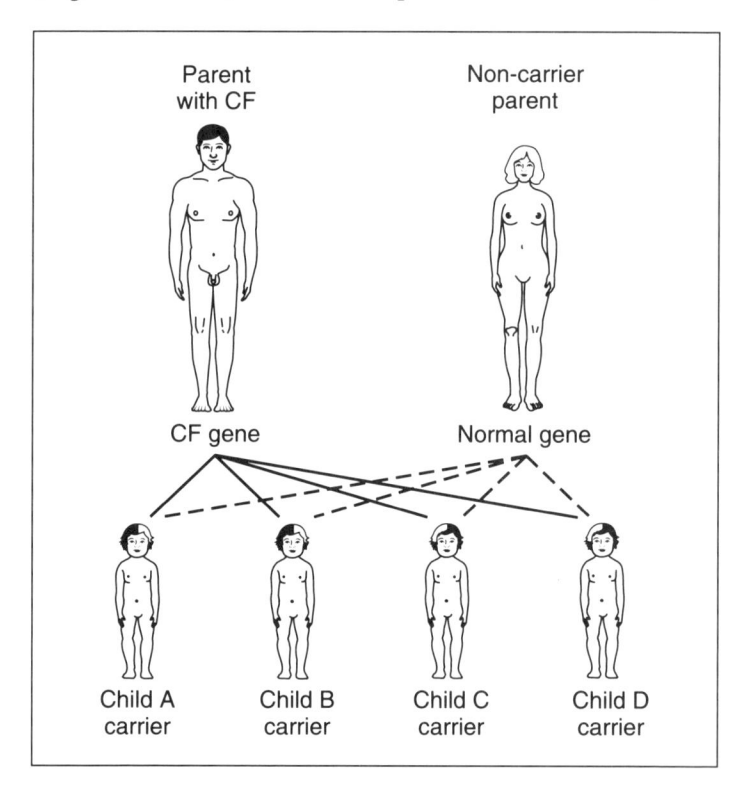

FIGURE 6. *When one parent has cystic fibrosis and the other has no CF gene, all offspring will be carriers.*

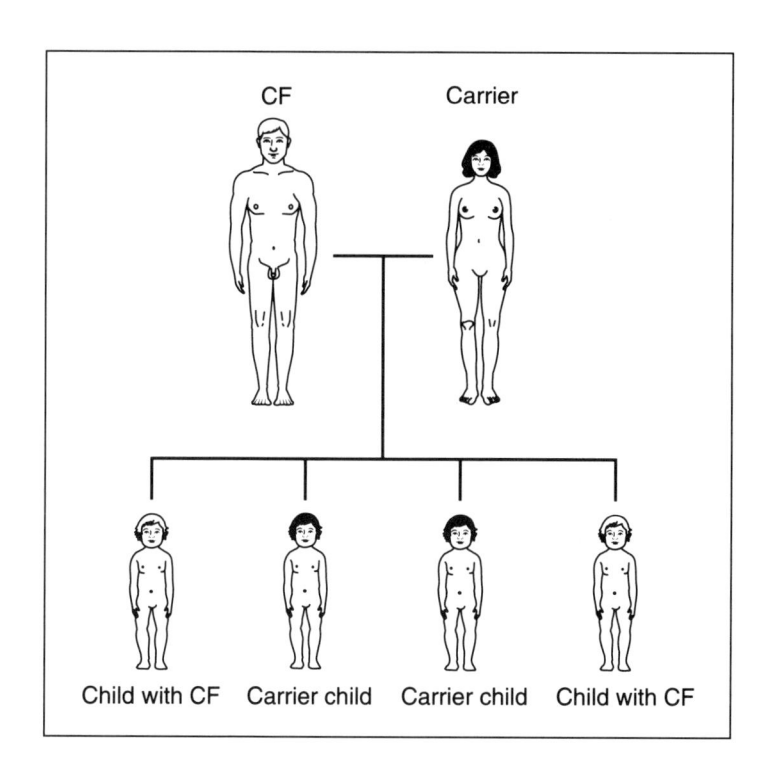

FIGURE 7. *The offspring of a person with cystic fibrosis and a carrier have a 50 percent chance of having CF. However, only 1 in 25 people are carriers. Therefore, the general risk of having a child with CF is only 1 in 50.*

none of the children that are born will have CF—but they will all be carriers. If one parent has CF and the other is a carrier, there is a 50 percent chance that a child will have CF and a 50 percent chance that the child will be a carrier. Two CF parents would have a child with cystic fibrosis.

These hereditary patterns hold true for large numbers of people. But in a particular real family, with just a few children, the assortment may not match the charts. For

INHERITING CF[4]

When both parents are carriers, there are four possibilities:

1. If a sperm with the CF gene combines with an egg with the CF gene, the child will have CF.

2. If a sperm with the CF gene combines with an egg without the CF gene, the child will be a CF carrier.

3. If a sperm without the CF gene combines with an egg with the CF gene, the child will be a CF carrier.

4. If a sperm without the CF gene combines with an egg without the CF gene, the child will not have CF and will not be a carrier.

example, if two CF carriers have four children, they won't necessarily include one child with CF, two carriers, and one child free of the CF gene. All four children might be carriers, or all might have CF; or all four might be free of the gene—or any other combination.

If parents have one child with CF, that does not mean that the next one will or will not have CF. The odds apply all over again for each pregnancy. And unlike some hereditary diseases, cystic fibrosis is just as likely to occur in either males or females.

8
THE CYSTIC FIBROSIS GENE

THE RACE TO FIND THE CYSTIC FIBROSIS GENE

Several different teams of researchers around the world worked for nearly a decade to unravel the mystery of the cystic fibrosis gene. Finally, in August of 1989, it was announced that Lap-Chee Tsui and John R. Riordan of the Hospital for Sick Children in Toronto, working with Francis Collins of the University of Michigan and their colleagues, had identified the gene that is responsible for causing cystic fibrosis.[1]

The battle had been a long one, made possible by smaller discoveries throughout the 1980s. In the early 1980s Richard C. Boucher and his colleagues at the University of North Carolina noticed that cells taken from the lungs of CF patients contained large amounts of sodium and chloride ions. This discovery was not really very surprising. Back in the 1950s doctors knew something was wrong with the way salt (sodium chloride) was transported in the sweat glands, because the sweat of CF patients had too much salt in it. But the University of North Carolina researchers believed that this sodium and chloride imbalance could explain why the mucus was so thick in the lungs of patients with cystic fibrosis. They and another research team at the University of California, led by Paul Quinton, found that the outer membranes of epithelial cells in people with CF would not allow chloride ions to leave.[2] So salt concentrations built up inside the epithelial cells. Normally, when there is too much water in cells, water from their surroundings—in this case, the mucous coating—tends to flow into them to restore the balance. But this cannot happen in the faulty CF cells.

In the mid-1980s Raymond Frizell at the University of Alabama and Michael Welsh of the University of Iowa and their colleagues concluded that the protein channel that normally transports chloride ions and water through cell membranes is not opened properly in people with CF.[3] This unknown protein might be the key to the problem, the product of the faulty gene that causes CF.

Scientists were gaining a better understanding of the disease, but no one knew what the malfunctioning protein looked like, and they didn't know where to begin to look for the gene that caused the protein to be made incorrectly.

HOW TO TRACK DOWN A GENE

There were several different approaches scientists could take to try to figure out which gene was the cause of cystic fibrosis. One way was to use *forward genetics*. In this method scientists study the protein that a gene produces. They map the amino acid sequence of the protein chain and then can easily figure out the sequence of base pairs in DNA that would produce that amino acid sequence in the gene's protein product. Then they search the chromosomes for a gene with this sequence. Scientists used forward genetics to locate the sickle-cell anemia gene. They knew that the sickle-cell gene produced hemoglobin molecules that were not formed properly. After mapping out the amino acid sequence of the hemoglobin molecule, they knew what the sickle-cell gene should look like.

But for most of the four thousand human disorders that are known to be caused by defective genes, scientists aren't sure exactly what causes the disease. This was true of cystic fibrosis. Scientists suspected that a defective protein was responsible, but they didn't know what it looked like.

Some scientists were working on trying to figure out which protein was supposed to be the chloride channel. By mid-1989, Qais Al-Awqati and his colleagues at Columbia University in New York had narrowed down the protein to one of several possibilities.[4]

Meanwhile other labs were using *positional cloning*— searching through the chromosomes for a gene without knowing its actual sequence. This method works very well when researchers know which chromosome to look at. But at first no one knew which of the twenty-three chromosome pairs was carrying the CF gene. Imagine the job of sorting through three billion base pairs, looking for a particular gene when you don't know where it is or what the protein it produces looks like!

Researchers launched a search for chromosome "markers" using the DNA from families with cystic fibrosis. It has been found that the chromosomes of family members have a number of particular DNA patterns in common. Some of these characteristic patterns, or markers, happen to be located near the genes for particular traits—like blue eyes or the faulty protein responsible for CF. Genes that are close together on a chromosome are often inherited together. So, if the scientists could find markers that nearly all the people with cystic fibrosis had, they would know that the marker was probably very close to the cystic fibrosis gene. Then they would look between the new markers to narrow down the search again and again until they found the CF gene.

The researchers used a technique called *chromosome*

walking or *gene walking* to move along strands of DNA piece by piece. With three billion possible base pairs to check through, this can take a lot of time, and it can sometimes be quite difficult, because there are often huge stretches of DNA that are hard to get past.

Bob Williamson at St. Mary's Hospital in London, and Ray White of the University of Utah and their colleagues were working with gene mapping using markers. So was Lap-Chee Tsui in Toronto, working with Collaborative Research in Massachusetts. Late in 1985 both groups announced at the same time that the cystic fibrosis gene was somewhere on the seventh chromosome (Figure 8).

In 1986 seven research groups pooled all their information and concluded that the gene was between the markers that Williamson and White had determined. But there were still 1.5 million base pairs to look through. Williamson's lab came up with a possibility for the cystic fibrosis gene in 1987. Everyone thought that his lab had won the race, but after six months of testing it was concluded that it wasn't the right gene after all, just a close neighbor.

Tsui meanwhile had joined forces with Francis Collins at the University of Michigan, who was an expert at *chromosome jumping*, a process that greatly speeded up the searching process. Using this technique, the researchers could jump over 100,000 bases at a time and could continue looking further down the chromosome. "To find the cystic fibrosis gene by 'walking' would have taken at least eighteen years," Collins said.[5] In June 1989 Tsui, Riordan, and Collins finally isolated the CF gene. Chromosome jumping had allowed them to find it only two years after the researchers teamed up.

The CF gene is spread out over a long stretch of DNA—250,000 base pairs! Not all cases of CF are caused by the same genetic defect. So far researchers have found about 300 different defects on the CF gene.[6] Nearly 70

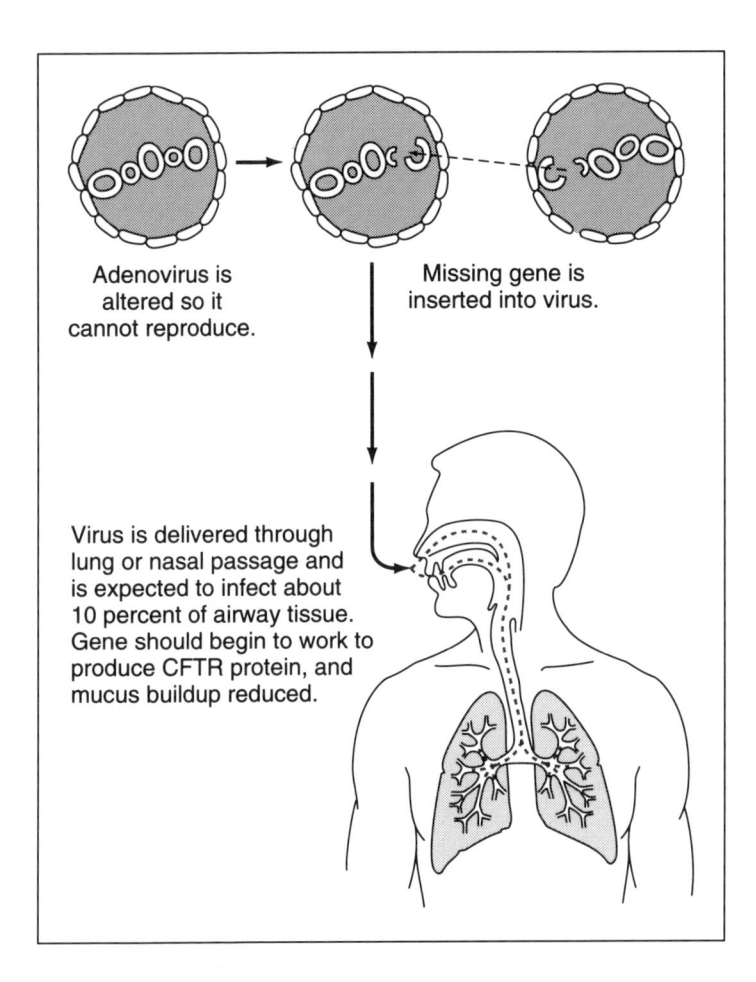

FIGURE 8. *Researchers are developing a technique that uses adenoviruses, which cause colds, to deliver CFTR genes to lung cells.*

percent of all CF cases, however, are due to a single flaw, which involves just three base pairs. Four defects make up 85 percent of all CF cases. The other 15 percent of the flaws are much rarer. In fact, some defects are so rare that they occur only in one specific family or in one individual person.

THE CFTR PROTEIN

A normal cystic fibrosis gene tells the body to make a very large protein, which is made up of 1,480 amino acids. The protein lodges in the cell membranes, and scientists believe that it regulates or controls the amount of chloride ions that go in and out of cells. For this reason it was named CFTR, or *cystic fibrosis transmembrane regulator*.

Regulating chloride ions is an important part of the water-balance system in the body that makes sure cells don't dry out, or get so full of water that they burst.

Researchers believe that the protein works in two ways to regulate chloride ions. One part of the CFTR protein acts as an *ion channel*—a gate for chloride ions to pass through, into, and out of the cell. Another part of the protein controls the gate, deciding whether it should be open or closed. This is very unusual. Before the CFTR protein was discovered, scientists had never seen protein molecules that act as both the gate and the gatekeeper. Dr. John R. Riordan of the Hospital for Sick Children in Toronto, one of the researchers studying the chloride ion regulator, commented on how unusual the discovery was. "We've seen ion channels and we've seen regulators of ion channels, but we've never observed them both in one protein before."[7]

In cystic fibrosis the flaw in the genetic instructions produces a protein that does not work properly. A malfunctioning gatekeeping protein does not open and shut properly, and chloride ions cannot pass out of the cells.

In 70 percent of cystic fibrosis cases, a single amino acid (phenylalanine) is missing about one-third of the way along the CFTR protein chain, at position 508. The amino acid is missing at a place on the gene where ATP—the cell's source of energy—usually binds. Scientists believe that without the missing amino acid, ATP cannot join up with the protein, and chloride cannot be transported through the cell membrane.

The passage of chloride ions is very closely linked with the passage of sodium ions (sodium and chloride combined make up table salt, or sodium chloride). The cells do not secrete enough chloride ions, and they also absorb too many sodium ions, causing an imbalance in both chloride and sodium. This causes a water imbalance, as water is drawn into the cells to try to correct the salt imbalance. This causes the mucus to become thick and sticky, like jelly.

WHAT GOES WRONG WITH THE CFTR PROTEIN?

Researchers believe that a portion of the protein (called the R-domain) produced by a defective gene acts like a molecular "flap" which blocks the channel for chloride ions to pass out of the cell.

Other researchers think that mutations in the CF gene may prevent the CFTR protein from being processed properly, resulting in an incomplete protein that does not reach the cell surface. So CF may result from a lack of the protein rather than its faulty functioning. Scientists are still trying to explain the seemingly contradictory findings.[8]

9
THE TESTING CONTROVERSY

Living with cystic fibrosis is a lifetime ordeal—even now, when improved treatments are bringing that lifetime closer and closer to the normal span. Frank Deford, who wrote a poignant book about Alex, his courageous young daughter with CF, notes that psychologists have found that children with a chronic disease typically assume that the illness is a punishment. And the therapies for CF may seem to add to the punishment.[1] It can be an agonizing trial for a parent, too. "Two thousand times I had to beat my sick child," writes Deford, referring to the chest therapy routine, "—and in the end, for what?"[2] Few parents would want to go through an ordeal like that. That is why doctors now advise that family members of a CF patient be tested to determine whether they are carrying the CF gene. That way they can decide whether to risk having a child with cystic fibrosis.

TO TEST OR NOT TO TEST?

But what about screening the general population to test for CF carriers? Since the gene is relatively common, should people be aware of whether or not they can pass the disease on to their children?

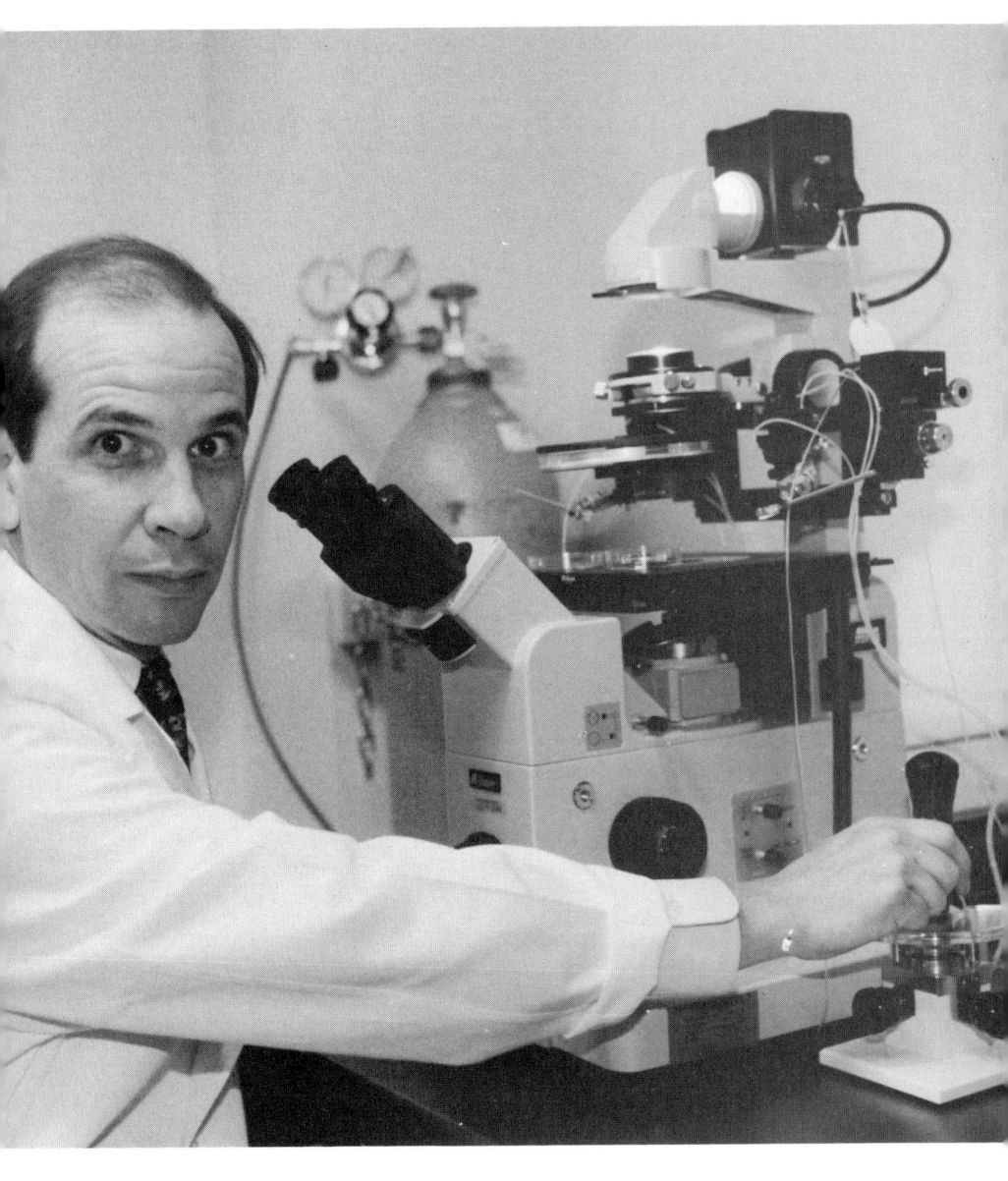

Dr. Mark Hughes is a researcher at the Baylor College of Medicine in Houston. He and a British doctor have developed a genetic test to detect the presence of cystic fibrosis before birth.

It is believed that about twelve million Americans are cystic fibrosis carriers. (Researchers estimate that somewhere between one in twenty to one in twenty-five Americans carry the defective gene.[3]) We cannot tell that a person is a CF carrier by looking for symptoms, because there won't be any. But now that scientists know where the CF gene is, a blood test can usually determine whether or not a person has the CF gene.

Genetic testing can relieve worries, in addition to pointing out possible dangers. For example, both prospective parents may discover that they are not CF carriers, and therefore they have no chance of having a child with cystic fibrosis. If only one of them is carrying the CF gene, their children, too, will all be healthy. But each child will have a 50 percent chance of inheriting a CF gene and thus of being a carrier. That is something that might be useful for the children to know when they grow up.

Some health experts believe there should be wide-scale screening for cystic fibrosis. They believe that all those thinking about having children should be tested. When both husband and wife are carriers, alternative birthing options should be explored, such as adoption, or the use of donor sperm or eggs.

HIGH-TECH BIRTH

In vitro fertilization, in which eggs and sperm are combined in a laboratory culture dish, permits embryos to be tested for the disease at very early stages of development, when they consist of just four cells. (Removing one of the cells for testing does not harm the other three, which can develop into a normal child.) Embryos that have passed the test are implanted into the mother's uterus to develop there. In 1992, doctors in England announced that a couple who were CF carriers had given birth to a healthy baby girl from an embryo that was produced and tested in vitro.

Many people are against wide-scale screening. It is much easier to determine whether other family members are carriers when a person has CF, than to test the general public. Remember, many different mutations on the CF gene can cause the disease. If a family member has CF, the specific mutation on the CF gene can be identified. Then other family members can be tested for this particular pattern. But for the general public, the current tests are only about 95 percent accurate, because of the other possible mutations the test does not detect. That means that even if a couple gets a negative result, there is a one in twenty chance that the test was wrong, and they could still have a child with cystic fibrosis.

Even if both parents turn out to be carriers, statistically there is still a a three out of four chance that their baby will *not* have the disease. With odds like those, some couples would decide to go ahead and try to have a child, especially since prenatal tests can tell, long before birth, whether the child is healthy.

Even the best testing programs turn up false positives—that is, the test indicates they are carrying the faulty gene when they really do not. Some experts believe that if wide-scale testing is done, perhaps one in one thousand could be falsely identified as being at risk for having a child with cystic fibrosis.[4]

Francis Collins, one of the discoverers of the cystic fibrosis gene, says, "Just because we technically know how to test for the DNA, doesn't mean we are ready to do this on a large scale." He and others feel it would worry and upset people needlessly in most cases.[5]

University of Wisconsin pediatricians Benjamin Wilfond and Norman Fost point out that people with false positives may alter their decision to have a child, and in addition, Fost points out, those identified as CF carriers may suffer other repercussions. "There might be loss of insurability or discrimination in employment."[6]

Wide-scale screening would also cost the country a lot

of money. About five million couples would have to be handled, costing at least $500 million. This would be about $2.2 million for each cystic fibrosis birth avoided. Wilfond and Fost suggest that the test be made available only for those with a family history of CF or for those who ask for it. In such cases, testing may be well worth the cost. According to a survey by the U.S. Congress in 1992, the cost of caring for a child with mild to severe cystic fibrosis ranged from $8,500 to $46,000 each year![7]

ETHICAL DILEMMAS

There is another, deeper ethical problem involved in the testing dilemma. Is it morally right to take steps to avoid the birth of a child with CF, perhaps even to abort an embryo found to be carrying a double dose of the gene? For all the pain and struggle, how many cystic fibrosis patients would have chosen not to be born?—especially now that improved treatments have greatly improved their chances for life and there is hope of finding a cure, perhaps within their lifetime! People disagree about the answers to these questions, and even about whether there are any "right answers."

In 1991 it was announced that the National Center for Human Genome Research would give out grants totaling $1 million to conduct voluntary testing for cystic fibrosis carriers. The test requires just a drop of blood. This testing program is "seen as precedent setting with wide application. We'll do pilot studies to see what is the best way to do it," says Eric T. Juengst, the center's director in charge of a program on the ethical, legal and social implications of mapping the human genome.[8] This project is the first application of what may eventually be wide-scale screening for genes.

The Human Genome Project is a fifteen-year project

that is under way to locate and identify all the human genes. The benefits of knowing the human genome are numerous. Researchers will have a major key into curing many diseases that harm and kill people. But genetic testing continues to be a subject of debate and controversy.

10
FUTURE TREATMENT OF CYSTIC FIBROSIS

The first thing nine-year-old Shiloh Avery said after her operation was "Mom, I'm hungry!" But then she whispered in amazement, "I can *breathe!*" Now she could look forward to many dreams coming true—riding her bike, climbing on the jungle gym at the playground, and going fishing with her father. Simple pleasures like these, which most children take for granted, had been only a dream for Shiloh because ever since birth she had been suffering from cystic fibrosis. The damage to her lungs was so severe that she had to go everywhere with an oxygen tank and a breathing tube. But now she had received a double lung transplant at St. Louis Children's Hospital, and her new lungs were working perfectly.[1]

Lung transplants are still a very experimental treatment—so new that doctors are not yet sure how long the recipients will survive. (As of 1992, about 70 percent of the thirteen hundred patients who had received lung transplants had survived for at least a year.)[2] Transplants are used as a last resort for CF patients who are not doing well on the standard treatments. They work because the cells in the new lungs have normal genes and thus do not become clogged with thick mucus. But this is not a "cure" for cystic fibrosis, or even a treatment that can be used

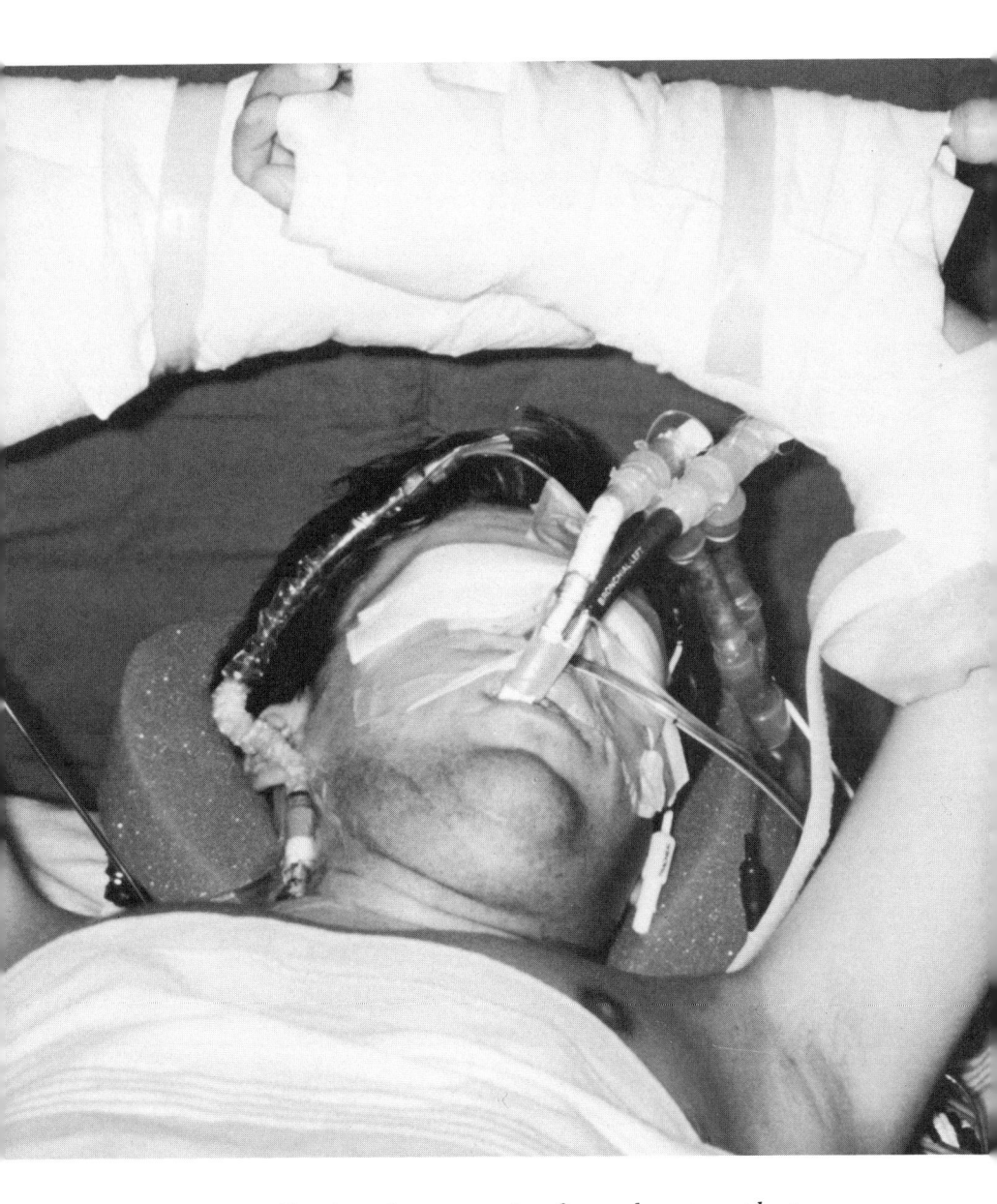

A cystic fibrosis patient recovering from a lung transplant. When a patient's lungs become severely infected, a lung transplant is the only hope for survival.

very widely. For every CF patient who is helped by a lung transplant, someone—the lung donor—has died.

Researchers all over the world are trying to develop better treatments and even cures for CF. These new types of treatments are being tested at many of the Cystic Fibrosis Foundation care centers around the country.

For new drugs to be approved for use in humans, drug companies must conduct extensive tests first with animals, and then in clinical trials with humans. The Cystic Fibrosis Foundation works with drug companies to speed up the process of finding new drug treatments by allowing promising drugs to be used in the care centers on cystic fibrosis patients. "The companies provide the much-needed funding to move new drugs to the marketplace more quickly than ever before. . . . People with CF can benefit from the new treatments as well as be pioneers in research," said Dr. Robert J. Beall, Executive Vice President for Medical Affairs at the Cystic Fibrosis Foundation.[3]

The Cystic Fibrosis Foundation is involved in more than a dozen different clinical trials. Four major areas of treatment are being tested:

1. thinning the mucus
2. reducing inflammation in the lungs
3. reducing bacterial infections in the lungs
4. treating body organs affected by CF

THINNING THE MUCUS

One of the reasons the mucus of cystic fibrosis patients is so sticky is that it contains high concentrations of DNA. When infections develop in the lungs and other passages in the body because of the mucus buildup, white blood cells are sent in to fight the infection. When the white blood cells die they release their DNA into the mucus. But this makes the mucus even thicker and stringier. A vicious circle develops, and conditions get worse and worse. The thick mucus makes the environment in the lungs even better for bacteria to grow, and it also prevents antibiotics from working properly.

Researchers headed by Ronald G. Crystal of the National Heart, Lung and Blood Institute found that a drug called DNase (deoxyribonuclease), which is made by Genentech Inc. in South San Francisco, California, may help cystic fibrosis patients to clear their lungs of the dangerous mucus. The drug is sprayed into patients' lungs as an aerosol, and it acts as a "molecular scissors" to chop up the thick mucus by breaking down the extra DNA outside the cells, without harming the DNA inside the cells. Dr. Crystal described the drug as acting "like Drano in chopping up and digesting the DNA."[4] This thins out the mucus and makes it easier for patients to clear air passages by coughing.

In a preliminary study of sixteen patients, Dr. Crystal found that "within twelve to twenty-four hours the patients report that they feel better and can do more,"[5] Eleven of sixteen patients had a noticeable improvement in their ability to breathe.

DNase is manufactured using gene splicing. It is a copy of a naturally occurring human enzyme. In the 1950s scientists experimented with DNase from cow pancreases, and over the years some studies concluded that inhaling cow DNase was helpful for people with lung infections. However, many had allergic reactions. In 1990 a research team at Genentech headed by Steven Shak announced that they had figured out the human DNase gene structure and cloned it. In the test tube DNase was found to reduce the thickness of CF patients' lung secretions tenfold. Dr. Crystal's team was then the first to use human DNase as an aerosol spray for cystic fibrosis patients. "It is not a cure, but there is no question it works," said Dr.

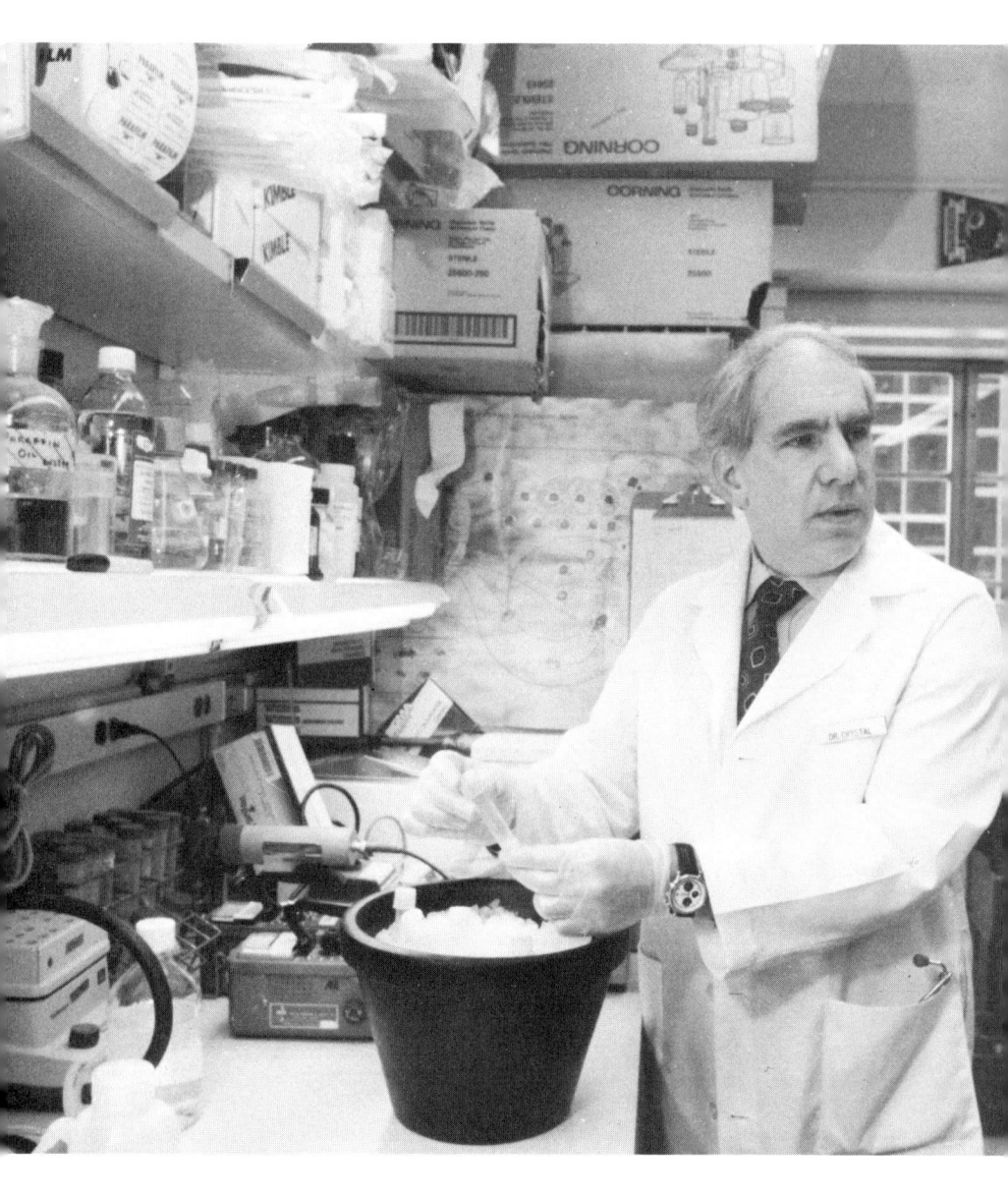

Dr. Ronald Crystal invented a drug called DNase, which thins mucus in the lungs, helping cystic fibrosis patients breathe easier and maintain healthier lungs.

Crystal.[6] The drug is being tested on humans, however, and by mid-1992 nine hundred patients at fifty hospitals throughout the country were using it. DNase may also be useful for patients with chronic bronchitis, emphysema, and pneumonia. The drug, marketed under the brand name Pulmozyme, is expected to be available in 1994, at an estimated cost of about $7000 a year per patient.

NORMALIZING THE WATER BALANCE

Researchers are trying to find drug treatments that will allow chloride ions to pass in and out of cells normally. One way of doing this is to find drugs that will bind to the CFTR protein and "unclog" the channel. Other drugs may be able to "convince" different channels present in the membranes to substitute for the jammed CFTR protein. Then these other channels could transport chloride ions as well as whatever they normally channel.

Phyllis Gardner of Stanford University is studying how the epithelial cells in the airway react to calcium. She has found that increasing the amount of calcium inside the cells helps chloride ions to be transported more normally.[8]

In the early 1990s researchers at the University of North Carolina found two drugs that could fix the salt imbalance. In 1990, Michael R. Knowles and colleagues at the University of North Carolina found that *amiloride*, a blood pressure medicine, helped cells absorb sodium more normally when it was breathed into the lungs in an aerosol form.

In 1991 the UNC research team headed by Dr. Knowles and Richard C. Boucher also found that they could increase the amount of chloride secreted from cells to more normal levels by using two naturally occurring substances, ATP and UTP (adenosine triphosphate and uridine triphosphate). These substances, which are found naturally in the cells of our bodies, are called *nucleotides*. In addition to serving as DNA building blocks, they are used for energy to power the cells. Dr. Boucher believes that ATP works not on the defective CFTR protein but on a different membrane protein, called the *purinergic receptor*.[9]

Researchers are hopeful that a combination of the two treatments may help to normalize the flow of water in and out of the cells in the lungs, thus preventing the buildup of mucus. In early tests the researchers have found the treatment to be effective, but more tests are needed to make sure that the drugs can be safely breathed into the lungs. This treatment doesn't cure the disease, but it may help prevent one of the most harmful effects.

Dr. Knowles stated that "ultimately our goal would be to give these drugs [amiloride and triphosphate nucleotides] in combination at a very early age to protect the airways." This may help prevent lung damage which most often causes CF victims to die early.[10] Dr. Knowles added that the drugs could at least "keep them healthy until another therapy comes along."[11]

PROTEIN DELIVERY

An even more obvious way of correcting the flow of chloride ions is to replace the defective protein with normal CFTR protein. Using this future treatment, called *protein delivery*, the normal protein would be sprayed into lung cell membranes of cystic fibrosis patients. The normal protein could then channel chloride ions.

The only problem is that scientists would need a lot of the protein. Researchers at Genzyme Corp in Framingham, Massachusetts, were able to load laboratory mice with healthy CFTR genes and get the mice to produce the normal protein. In the future, scientists may be able to get the large amount of proteins needed to treat cystic fibrosis from living "pharmacies" like these laboratory mice, or from cows or goats.[12] The CFTR protein is produced in the animals' milk and thus could easily be collected in large amounts. Robert J. Beall of the Cystic Fibrosis Foundation (CFF) described the idea by saying "basically we're talking about a four-legged manufacturing plant."[13]

SIMPLIFYING THE CFTR PROTEIN

The CF gene and the protein it produces are unusually large, but a lot is just "filler" material. It would be much easier to synthesize if only the important parts were included. Researchers are studying the CFTR protein one segment at a time to try and determine which sections are absolutely necessary for the protein to function properly. They are doing this by removing portions of the normal gene. This changes the genetic instructions slightly. Then researchers study the protein produced by the changed gene to see if it still channels chloride ions properly. This way they can determine which sections are really needed and which aren't.

REDUCING INFLAMMATION

When an infection develops in the body, inflammation usually occurs as part of the body's reaction. *Neutrophils* are a type of white blood cell that build up in the lungs as part of the inflammatory response. However, these neutrophils release a protein called *elastase* which can damage lung tissue. A drug called alpha-1 antitrypsin works to prevent this from happening. This drug reduces both the damage caused by elastase and the accumulation of neutrophils.[14]

SLPI, Secretory Leukoprotease Inhibitor, is another

drug that is being tested to prevent elastase from damaging the body. CFF is working with the pharmaceutical company Synergen in Boulder, Colorado, to test SLPI. A drug manufactured by ICI Pharmaceuticals of Wilmington, Delaware, also attacks elastases, and clinical trials are underway.

Ibuprofen, an anti-inflammatory drug used for headaches and muscle aches, is also being tested by CFF and Upjohn Company to reduce the destructive effects of elastase.

TREATING BACTERIAL INFECTIONS

Other researchers are searching for more effective antibiotic treatments. At the University of Washington in Seattle a three-year study concluded that an antibiotic called *tobramycin* was effective in a highly concentrated aerosol form. The antibiotic was useful in killing the hard-to-get-rid-of pseudomonas bacteria. After treatment, the number of bacteria in patients' lungs decreased from one hundred to ten thousand times![15]

ORGAN-SPECIFIC DRUGS

Ursodeoxycholic acid appears to help prevent liver disease in people with CF by helping bile to flow better. Thick bile can cause the liver to become enlarged. European scientists did much of the groundwork toward testing the drug.

AN ANIMAL MODEL

In 1992, a research team at the University of North Carolina reported a new advance that will be a big help in learning more about how CF develops and also aid in developing new tests and treatments. Many human diseases also occur in animals, and researchers are able to study them and try out new treatments without the risk of harming human patients. But there are no animals that naturally develop CF. The North Carolina team produced mutant CFTR genes in mouse cells, then inserted the changed cells into mouse embryos. The mice that grew from these embryos were bred to produce a line of CF carriers, called "knockout mice." When the knockout mice were mated, their offspring that inherited two mutant genes developed some symptoms similar to those in humans with CF. Nutritional problems made them smaller than other mice of the same age, and their intestines became clogged with thick mucus. Their lungs also showed some of the changes observed in the lungs of human CF patients.

These knockout mice are already giving researchers new insights into how CF does its damage and permitting them to test new treatments. Richard Boucher, a member of the North Carolina team, describes a study of amiloride, a drug to regulate salt secretion. Testing the drug on fifteen patients gave promising results but took a year and a half and cost $700,000. Tests on mice are much faster and cheaper and can also show whether the drug will be effective in preventing lung damage before it develops. Without the mice, Boucher says, "you would have to do that with kids. And it's not only hard to give an unknown drug to a kid, but you're asking about something that will happen five years down the pike. It's a long study."[16]

HOPE FOR THE FUTURE

The new therapies offer much hope for helping people with CF to live healthier lives. "We have every reason to believe that many of the new therapies now under investigation will significantly lengthen the lifespan and improve the quality of life for people with CF," said Robert Beall. "Due in large part to extensive clinical trials, progress in CF treatment continues to be phenomenal."[17]

11
GENE THERAPY: HOPE FOR A CURE

Eleven-year-old Katie used to hate recess. When she tried to run she couldn't keep up with the other kids and soon started to cough. But now she is taking DNase treatments that break up the thick mucus that was choking her lungs. "I can run without getting tired," she says delightedly.[1] But the treatment is not a cure. Katie and her sixteen-year-old sister, Jennifer, who also has cystic fibrosis, have to keep on taking DNase regularly, and every few months they have to go back to Children's Hospital in Boston for a few weeks to have their lungs cleaned out. A real cure would mean an end to all those bothersome treatments. Scientists now hope that cystic fibrosis will be cured soon, through a technique called *gene therapy*.

REPLACING DEFECTIVE GENES

Since cystic fibrosis is caused by a defective gene, many scientists believe the most logical way to "cure" it is to replace the defective gene in patients with the disease. If CF patients had a normal gene instead, their bodies would produce the right protein, and their lungs would not become filled with fluid.

In 1990 several different researchers were able to insert normal copies of the CFTR gene into epithelial cells from cystic fibrosis patients in a culture dish. When they did so, chloride ions were transported normally in and out of the cells—the cells were "cured." The technique worked both on lung cells and on pancreas cells.[2]

Researchers became excited about the idea of using gene therapy to treat or cure cystic fibrosis. The only problem was how to do it.

Normally, gene therapy involves removing a sample of defective cells from a patient and inserting a healthy gene into the cell samples. Then the cells are reinserted back into the patient. The altered cells multiply, and the necessary amount of the normal protein is produced. However, this is not possible with cystic fibrosis. It would be impossible to remove and reinsert cells into all parts of the lungs.

The perfect solution would be to find a "vehicle" to which the gene could be attached (Figure 9). The vehicle would then travel to the places where it is needed, and deposit the gene. At the National Heart, Lung, and Blood Institute in Bethesda, Maryland, researcher Ronald Crystal thought that a cold virus (called an adenovirus) would be a suitable vehicle.

Viruses infect cells by injecting their own DNA into a cell. If a copy of a normal CFTR gene were attached to the virus's DNA, it would pass along the CFTR gene, too. Adenoviruses seemed a good choice because they hone in on the delicate linings of our respiratory system. Once the normal CFTR gene was inside the cell, it might produce enough of the vital chloride channel protein to essentially cure the lungs of a person with cystic fibrosis.

Of course, doctors wouldn't want to make their patients sick to get them better—adenoviruses cause colds, bronchitis, and other respiratory infections. Fortunately it is rather easy to remove the genes that allow the virus to multiply. Then it can't cause a cold.

In 1991, Dr. Crystal used an altered cold virus to insert a healthy human CFTR gene into the lung cells of cotton rats. Animals don't get cystic fibrosis, so it wasn't possible to "cure" the rats. But the experiment was a success. The rat lung cells did indeed pick up the human CFTR gene and began to produce normal human chloride channel protein. The researchers were afraid the effect would be very temporary, because lung cells live only for a few weeks or months and are quickly replaced by new ones—which might not contain the corrective genes. But six weeks after the experiment began, cells from the rats' lungs were still producing human chloride channels. By early 1992, researchers had successfully inserted the gene into the epithelial cells lining the lungs of hundreds of rats, and the normal CFTR protein was produced for up to four months.

In the future, patients may simply use an inhaler to get the genetically altered cold virus into their lungs. Because normal lung cells are shed periodically, the treatment may have to be repeated every few months, though.

"I have no doubt at all that if we were to put this in the lungs of patients, we would correct the cystic fibrosis now." Dr. Crystal has said.[3] He is working together with more than a dozen other scientists around the world on the project, testing the procedure in rats and monkeys. In 1993 his team and researchers at the University of Pennsylvania began testing the gene therapy technique on human cystic fibrosis patients.[4]

POSSIBLE BARRIERS TO GENE THERAPY

Gene therapy researchers are watching out for many possible problems. First of all, they want to make sure that the virus vehicle will not affect any other tissues beside the lungs.

Because viruses are very easily spread from one person

to another, the researchers want to make sure that other people will not become infected with the virus from a treated patient.

Researchers need to make sure that the virus will not regain its ability to multiply. The patient might have a similar adenovirus lying inactive in his lungs from a previous infection, or may be infected with one during treatment, and the altered adenovirus could receive the missing reproductive genes from the normal adenovirus. If it does, the adenovirus could become uncontrollable. It could start dividing rapidly, producing tremendous amounts of the protein.

Fortunately, researchers have found that excess amounts of the chloride channel protein do not seem to be harmful to the body. But the spreading virus could also cause a serious respiratory infection.

Moreover, the virus might trigger an immune response. The patient's body would build up antibodies against the virus, so that the next time the adenovirus was sprayed into the lungs, these defenders would be sent out to kill the adenovirus before it could deliver the normal CF gene. This would make future treatments ineffective. Even worse, the spreading virus could cause an inflammation in the lungs, which would be extremely bad for the patient. Dr. Crystal points out that, "I'm sure we could do it safely once, but I'm not sure what would happen the second time."[5]

It has been found that the CFTR protein is present not only in epithelial cells but also in cells buried deeper in the lungs. Researchers feared that gene therapy might not work if it affected only the epithelial cells. However, they were greatly encouraged when a University of North Carolina research team found that chloride was secreted normally when only 10 percent of the cells were corrected with the normal CF gene. This means that only a small proportion of the cells may need to be corrected in order for the lungs to work properly.[6]

SEARCHING FOR SOLUTIONS

Even if researchers find impassable stumbling blocks to working with adenoviruses, other researchers are developing different ways of transporting the CFTR gene into airway cells.

One research team at the National Institutes of Health directed by Dr. Barrie Carter is using adeno-associated viruses to deliver the genes. These viruses target lung cells just as adenoviruses do, but they don't cause colds or other diseases.[7]

Several research teams are joining CFTR genes with proteins or lipids which will make the passage into airway cells easier. At Vanderbilt University and the University of Cincinnati, for example, researchers are surrounding the CF gene with fat globules called *liposomes*. When sprayed into the lungs the globules attach to epithelial cells, transferring the genes to the cells.[8]

At the University of North Carolina researchers are working to attach the normal CF gene to the outside of a virus. When a virus is altered to carry a gene inside there is a limit to how much the virus can carry. When a "load" is attached to the outside of the virus, much more can be carried.[9]

Delivering replacement genes to the lungs, of course, would not solve the whole problem of CF. Although the lungs are the most important organs to treat, ways may also have to be found to deliver working genes to the pancreas and liver, as well. These are likely to present even more challenging problems. Gene therapy is one of the most exciting avenues for researchers, though, because it offers the possibility of not just a treatment, but a cure. "We believe that this provides us with the unique opportunity to reverse the course of the disease. If this can work in humans we have the potential to stop the deaths caused by this disease," says Dr. Robert Beall of the Cystic Fibrosis Foundation.[10]

In 1991 a person with a rare immune disorder was treated with gene therapy. Scientists all over the world were excited because this was the first human treatment with gene therapy. Gene therapy experts around the world have begun to concentrate their efforts on cystic fibrosis gene therapy because many believe that CF is the most promising area to pursue in this new branch of science.

12
LIVING WITH CYSTIC FIBROSIS

People are concerned when someone they love becomes ill. But when a child is sick with the measles or the flu, a family knows the child will soon be better. When a family member has a chronic illness—one that won't just go away—it is not uncommon for many different emotional and psychological problems to develop for the patient, the family, and their friends.

WORRIES AND STRAINS

Everyone reacts to chronic illnesses differently, but there are many similarities. Parents feel concerned and worry about the child, because they don't know what to expect. Will their child be very sick? Will they be able to cope with all the attention the child will require? Children may feel angry that they have CF. Sometimes parents and other family members feel resentful of all the attention and time they have to devote to the child's illness. Parents may feel guilty knowing that CF is an inherited disease and that the child got it from them. Brothers and sisters may feel the parents are neglecting them and may resent the sick child. Parents may wonder how long their child will live, and both patient and family may have to come to accept the fact that the child may die from the disease.

It is completely normal for people to have these types of feelings, but they can sometimes cause real problems for families. The strain can cause marital conflicts, and change a family's whole way of life. A chronic illness can also drain a family's finances. The cystic fibrosis patient and family may need to work out many of the psychological, emotional, and social problems that arise by talking about the problems with friends, doctors, or counselors. In some communities families of cystic fibrosis patients have formed support groups to help each other cope with the disease. State services or a local Cystic Fibrosis Foundation chapter can help find solutions to the great financial strain a chronic illness can bring.

Many parents are not sure how to treat their chronically ill child. They may feel guilty about disciplining the child, for example. But doctors stress the need for parents to treat a chronically ill child as normally as possible. It is only natural for parents to want to protect their children, but overprotecting can stunt a child's emotional growth. Children with cystic fibrosis should be encouraged to be as self-reliant as they are able.

Parents should talk about CF with their child, as well as with other members of the family, so that everyone knows why special attention needs to be given to the child with cystic fibrosis.

ROUTINES FOR LIVING

Most families with a chronically ill child establish a normal routine that incorporates the child's treatments and other needs. Changes in that routine can sometimes be difficult, but they are often beneficial. Nursery school and day-care centers can be a rewarding experience for children with CF because it enables them to play with other children. But special arrangements must be made to make sure that enzyme supplements and other medications are taken, and that chest physical therapy is done. Special arrangements are also needed with babysitters, or when the child sleeps at a friend's home.

Very young children tend to accept the treatment routines as normal. But as they get older, they may rebel against the daily chest therapy routine. Parents may need to make treatment time pleasurable by watching television, listening to music, or playing games while chest physical therapy is being done, to keep the child motivated. Many brothers and sisters feel protective of the chronically ill child, and getting them involved in the home care routine can often help them feel better about the situation, as well as keep them from feeling neglected or left out.

Children may feel embarrassed or self-conscious about always coughing, or because they have to take medications or treatment while at school, or because of the strong odor of their bowel movements. They may be shorter or thinner than other children, and the disease may cause an enlargement of their fingertips. All these things can make the child feel different. This might be especially difficult for teenagers who normally already feel self-conscious. Teens may also rebel against being dependent on their parents for treatment and medications.

Life may seem difficult at times for families when a child has cystic fibrosis. But families know that all the time and trouble they go through is worth it because it makes their child's life better. CF does affect people both physically and emotionally, but people with CF can still have happy and fulfilling lives. And now for the first time, many families have great reason to hope that even more effective treatments, and possibly a cure, will arrive in time to save many who suffer from cystic fibrosis.

SOURCE NOTES

CHAPTER 1
1. Jack Jacoby, "A Determined Doctor, Both Healer and Patient, Wages a Lifelong Struggle Against Cystic Fibrosis," *People* (September 24, 1990), pp. 67–70.
2. James Cunningham and Lynn Taussig, *An Introduction to Cystic Fibrosis for Patients and Families* (Bethesda, Md.: The Cystic Fibrosis Foundation, 1989), pp. 2–3.
3. Associated Press, "New Treatment May Spare Cystic Fibrosis Victims," *The Star-Ledger* (August 22, 1991), p. 79.
4. James Cunningham and Lynn Taussig, *An Introduction to Cystic Fibrosis for Patients and Families* (Bethesda, Md.: The Cystic Fibrosis Foundation, 1991), p. 71.
5. Cystic Fibrosis Foundation, "Facts About CF" (fact sheet, March 1992.)

CHAPTER 2
1. Burton Shapiro and Ralph Heussner, Jr., *A Parent's Guide to Cystic Fibrosis* (Minneapolis, Minn.: University of Minnesota Press, 1991), p. 17.
2. James Cunningham and Lynn Taussig, *An Introduction to Cystic Fibrosis for Patients and Families* (Bethesda, Md.: The Cystic Fibrosis Foundation, 1991), p. 2.
3. Ann Harris and Maurice Super, *Cystic Fibrosis: The Facts* (New York: Oxford University Press, 1987), pp. 10–11.
4. Francis Collins, "Cystic Fibrosis: Molecular Biol-

ogy and Therapeutic Implications," *Science* (May 8, 1992), p. 774.
5. Ibid.

CHAPTER 3
1. Andrew Purvis, "Laying Siege to a Deadly Gene," *Time* (February 24, 1992), p. 60.
2. Encyclopaedia Britannica, "Cystic Fibrosis," *The New Encyclopaedia Brittanica* (Chicago: 1988), vol. 3, p. 832.
3. James Cunningham and Lynn Taussig, *An Introduction to Cystic Fibrosis for Patients and Families* (Bethesda, Md.: The Cystic Fibrosis Foundation, 1991), p. 14.
4. Ibid., p. 15.
5. Ibid., p. 86.
6. Joanne Silberner, "Following the Blueprint of a Deadly Inherited Disease," *U.S. News & World Report* (November 4, 1991), p. 73.

CHAPTER 4
1. Jacquie Gordon, *Give Me One Wish* (New York: W. W. Norton, 1988), p. 17.
2. A. William Holmes, "Cystic Fibrosis," *The World Book Encyclopedia* (Chicago: 1988), vol. 4, p. 1209.
3. Burton Shapiro and Ralph Heussner, Jr., *A Parent's Guide to Cystic Fibrosis* (Minneapolis, Minn.: University of Minnesota Press, 1991), p. 28.
4. Ann Harris and Maurice Super, *Cystic Fibrosis: The Facts* (New York: Oxford University Press, 1987), p. 18.
5. Burton Shapiro and Ralph Heussner, Jr., *A Parent's Guide to Cystic Fibrosis* (Minneapolis, Minn.: University of Minnesota Press, 1991), p. 32.
6. Ibid., p. 36.
7. Ibid.
8. James Cunningham and Lynn Taussig, *An Introduction to Cystic Fibrosis for Patients and Families* (Bethesda, Md.: The Cystic Fibrosis Foundation, 1991), p. 38.

9. Burton Shapiro and Ralph Heussner, Jr., *A Parent's Guide to Cystic Fibrosis* (Minneapolis, Minn.: University of Minnesota Press, 1991), p. 35.

CHAPTER 5

1. Christopher Wills, *Introns, Exons, and Talking Genes* (New York: Basic Books, 1991), p. 197.
2. Burton Shapiro and Ralph Heussner, Jr., *A Parent's Guide to Cystic Fibrosis* (Minneapolis, Minn.: University of Minnesota Press, 1991), p. 45.
3. McNeil Pharmaceutical, "Living With Cystic Fibrosis: Family Guide to Nutrition" (1990 booklet), p. 8.
4. Ibid., p. 7.
5. Ibid., p. 9.
6. James Cunningham and Lynn Taussig, *An Introduction to Cystic Fibrosis for Patients and Families* (Bethesda, Md.: The Cystic Fibrosis Foundation, 1991), p. 47.
7. Ibid., p. 49.
8. Burton Shapiro and Ralph Heussner, Jr., *A Parent's Guide to Cystic Fibrosis* (Minneapolis, Minn.: University of Minnesota Press, 1991), p. 51.
9. James Cunningham and Lynn Taussig, *An Introduction to Cystic Fibrosis for Patients and Families* (Bethesda, Md.: The Cystic Fibrosis Foundation, 1991), p. 50.
10. Ibid., p. 49.

CHAPTER 6

1. Burton Shapiro and Ralph Heussner, Jr., *A Parent's Guide to Cystic Fibrosis* (Minneapolis, Minn.: University of Minnesota Press, 1991), p. 56.
2. Ibid., p. 60.

CHAPTER 7

1. Roger Wolmuth, "Jimmy the Greek Faces His Longest Odds in a Family Fight for Life," *People* (October 26, 1981), pp. 28–31.

2. Kevin Davies, "The Search for the Cystic Fibrosis Gene," *New Scientist* (October 21, 1989), p. 55.

3. Francis Collins, "Cystic Fibrosis: Molecular Biology and Therapeutic Implications," *Science* (May 8, 1992), p. 774.

4. James Cunningham and Lynn Taussig, *An Introduction to Cystic Fibrosis for Patients and Families* (Bethesda, Md.: The Cystic Fibrosis Foundation, 1991), p. 6.

CHAPTER 8

1. Ron Arias, "A Medical Breakthrough Gives New Hope to David Reitz—And All Kids with Cystic Fibrosis," *People* (September 11, 1989), p. 84.

2. Kevin Davies, "Cystic Fibrosis: The Quest for a Cure," *New Scientist* (December 7, 1991), p. 30.

3. Kevin Davies, "The Search for the Cystic Fibrosis Gene," *New Scientist* (October 21, 1989), p. 55.

4. Ibid.

5. John Carey, "Tracking Down the Gene for Cystic Fibrosis," *Business Week* (Innovation, 1990), p. 52.

6. Roger Field, "Cystic Fibrosis Mutations Confuse Screening Issue," *Medical Tribune* (October 7, 1993), p. 8.

7. Natalie Angier, "Flawed 2-in-1 Protein Causes Cystic Fibrosis," *The New York Times* (February 26, 1991), p. C3.

8. Francis Collins, "Cystic Fibrosis: Molecular Biology and Therapeutic Implications," *Science* (May 8, 1992), p. 777.

CHAPTER 9

1. Frank Deford, *Alex: The Life of a Child* (New York: The Viking Press, 1983), p. 32.

2. Ibid., p. 33.

3. Cystic Fibrosis Foundation, "Facts About CF" (fact sheet, March, 1992); Christopher Wills, *Exons, Introns and Talking Genes* (New York: Basic Books, 1990), p. 195.

4. "Cystic Fibrosis: To Test or Not to Test?" *In Health* (Sept/Oct, 1990), p. 17.
5. Andrew Purvis, "Laying Siege to a Deadly Gene," *Time* (February 24, 1992), p. 61.
6. "Cystic Fibrosis: To Test or Not to Test?" *In Health* (Sept/Oct, 1990), p. 17.
7. Anita Cecchin, "Experts Debate Impact of Gene Test," *Medical Tribune* (October 22, 1972), p. 4.
8. The Baltimore Sun, "Cystic Fibrosis Gene Is Key Target," *The Bridgewater, N.J. Courier News* (July 21, 1991), p. A-7.

CHAPTER 10

1. William Plummer and Giovanna Breu, "A New Breath of Life," *People* (July 6, 1992), pp. 116–23.
2. Ibid., p. 116.
3. Cystic Fibrosis Foundation, "CF Therapies Explored Through Clinical Trials," July 1991 newsletter.
4. Marilyn Chase and Michael Waldholz, "Genentech Drug for Cystic Fibrosis Clears Safety Trial, *The Wall Street Journal* (March 19, 1992), p B6.
5. *The Los Angeles Times*, "Drug May Hold Key to Treatment of Cystic Fibrosis," *The Bridgewater, N.J. Courier News* (March 19, 1992), p. A-3.
6. Associated Press, "New Breath of Life: Protein Spray Unclogs Deadly Cystic Fibrosis Suffocator," *The Newark, N.J. Star-Ledger* (March 19, 1992), p. 3.
7. Lawrence M. Fisher, "Cystic Fibrosis Drug Wins Panel's Backing," *The New York Times* (August 10, 1993), p. C5.
8. Kevin Davies, "Cystic Fibrosis: The Quest for a Cure," *New Scientist* (December 7, 1991), p. 32.
9. Ibid.
10. K. A. Fackelmann, "Energy Duo Takes on CF's Chloride Defect," *Science News* (August 24, 1991), p. 117.
11. Andrew Purvis, "Laying Siege to a Deadly Gene," *Time* (February 24, 1992), p. 61.

12. Joanne Silberner, "Following the Blueprint of a Deadly Inherited Disease," *U.S. News & World Report* (November 4, 1991), p. 73.
13. Andrew Purvis, "Laying Siege to a Deadly Gene," *Time* (February 24, 1992), p. 61.
14. Kevin Davies, "Cystic Fibrosis: The Quest for a Cure," *New Scientist* (December 7, 1991), p. 34.
15. Cystic Fibrosis Foundation, "Scientists Explore Exciting New Drug Therapies," *Commitment* (February 1992 newsletter).
16. Marcia Barinaga, "Knockout Mice Offer First Animal Model for CF," *Science* (August 21, 1992), p. 1047.
17. Cystic Fibrosis Foundation, "CF Therapies Explored Through Clinical Trials," *Commitment* (July, 1991 newsletter).

CHAPTER 11

1. Mark Fischetti, "The Blossoming of Biotechnology," *Omni* (November 1992), p. 69.
2. "Fixing the Flaw of Cystic Fibrosis," *In Health* (Jan/Feb, 1991), p. 15.
3. Washington Post Wire Service, "Scientists May Be on Verge of Finding a Cure for Cystic Fibrosis," *The Newark, N.J. Star-Ledger* (January 10, 1992), p. 4.
4. Natalie Angier, "Cystic Fibrosis Experiment Hits a Snag," *The New York Times* (September 22, 1993), p. C12.
5. Jean Marx, "Gene Therapy for CF Advances," *Science* (January 17, 1992), p. 289.
6. Kevin Davies, "Cystic Fibrosis: The Quest for a Cure," *New Scientist* (December 7, 1991), p. 33.
7. Cystic Fibrosis Foundation, "Gene Therapy for CF: A Progress Report," (February, 1992 newsletter), p. 1.
8. Ibid., p. 2.
9. Ibid.
10. Associated Press, "Gene Therapy May Tame Cystic Fibrosis," *The Bridgewater, N.J. Courier News* (January 10, 1992), p. A-3.

GLOSSARY

aerosol—a mist of tiny liquid droplets suspended in air.
alveolus (pl. alveoli)—a tiny air-filled cavity in the lungs.
amniocentesis—a method of prenatal genetic testing using cells collected from the amniotic fluid surrounding the fetus inside the womb.
bronchial drainage (BD)—a form of physical therapy in which the chest is pounded from several directions to help drain mucus from the lungs.
bronchiectasis—a condition in which the bronchi are weak and stretched out.
bronchioles—the smallest of the air tubes leading into the lungs.
bronchodilator—a drug that widens the openings of the bronchial tubes.
bronchi (sing. bronchus)—the two air tubes that branch from the trachea.
carrier—a person who has a single gene for a recessive genetic disorder.
CFTR (cystic fibrosis transmembrane regulator) protein—a protein that controls the passage of chloride ions into and out of cells.
chest physiotherapy (CPT)—bronchial drainage.
chorionic villus biopsy—a method of prenatal diagnosis of genetic disorders using cells from the placenta.
chromosome—a thread-like structure, found in the cell nucleus, that contains the hereditary instructions for the body. A human being has 23 pairs of chromosomes.

chromosome walking, chromosome jumping—techniques used to determine the DNA structure of the genes in a chromosome.
cilia—tiny hair-like structures in the lining of the airways that help to clear out dust particles and bacteria from the lungs.
clubbing—enlargement of the tips of the fingers and toes.
cor pulmonale—enlargement of the right side of the heart.
cyst—a fluid-filled cavity.
decongestant—a drug that helps to shrink the swollen membranes lining the air passages.
diabetes mellitus—a disorder in which the hormones of the pancreas do not control the body's use of sugar properly and excess amounts build up in the blood.
DNA (deoxyribonucleic acid)—the chemical containing the body's hereditary instructions, spelled out in four kinds of building blocks called base pairs.
dominant trait—a hereditary trait that appears even when only one gene for it is present.
endocrine glands—structures that produce hormones, which help to coordinate and control body activities.
enzyme—a protein that helps to control chemical reactions in the body.
epithelium—cells lining the inside of the air passages and body organs.
exocrine glands—glands that secrete fluids through tiny tubes (ducts) to the body surface or into body organs. Sweat glands and the enzyme-producing part of the pancreas are exocrine glands.
gene—the unit of heredity: a portion of the DNA in the chromosomes that contains the instructions for producing a protein.
gene therapy—the transfer of genes to correct a genetic disorder by replacing missing or faulty genes.
genetic screening—wide-scale testing for genetic disorders.

hemoptysis—coughing up blood.
in vitro fertilization—combination of eggs and sperm in a laboratory culture dish to produce embryos.
inflammation—a reaction to tissue damage including pain, swelling, heat, and redness.
intravenous—delivered directly into the bloodstream.
knockout mice—specially bred mice with a defective CFTR gene that show some symptoms similar to cystic fibrosis in humans.
kyphosis—excessive curvature of the upper spine, which may result from the barrel-shaped chest that develops in people with CF.
liposomes—tiny fat globules.
malabsorption—failure of the body to absorb nutrients in food properly.
meconium ileus—blockage of the intestines in a newborn infant.
mucolytic—a drug that loosens the mucus so it can be coughed up more easily.
mucus—a fluid secreted by epithelial glands. It is normally thin and slippery, but in CF it is thick and sticky.
mutation—a change in a gene.
nasal polyps—growths of swollen mucous membrane in the lining of the nose.
pancreas—a gland that produces digestive enzymes and hormones (insulin and glucagon) that control the body's storage and use of sugar.
percussion—giving short, sharp blows to the lungs to help loosen mucus.
phlegm—mucus secreted by glands in the lining of the lungs and airways.
pneumothorax—a partial or complete collapse of the lungs due to leakage of air that becomes trapped between the lung and chest wall.
postural drainage (PD)—a synonym for bronchial drainage.

Pseudomonas aeruginosa—a bacterium causing lung infections in CF.
pulmonary function tests—tests used to evaluate lung function.
recessive trait—a hereditary trait that does not appear unless the person is carrying a pair of genes for it.
saline—saltwater.
sinusitis—infection of the lining of the sinuses (air spaces in the bones of the skull, which drain into the nasal cavity).
sputum—mucus and other substances coughed up from the lungs.
Staphylococcus aureus ("staph")—a bacterium causing lung infections in CF.
vital capacity—the amount of air that the lungs can move in and out.

FOR FURTHER READING

BOOKS

Cunningham, James and Lynn Taussig. *An Introduction to Cystic Fibrosis for Patients and Families.* Bethesda, Md.: The Cystic Fibrosis Foundation, 1989.

Deford, Frank. *Alex: The Life of a Child.* New York: The Viking Press, 1983.

Gordon, Jacquie. *Give Me One Wish.* New York: W. W. Norton, 1988.

Harris, Ann, and Maurice Super. *Cystic Fibrosis: The Facts.* New York: Oxford University Press, 1987.

Orenstein, David M. *Cystic Fibrosis: A Guide for Patient and Family* (New York: Raven Press, 1989).

Shapiro, Burton, and Ralph Heussner, Jr., *A Parent's Guide to Cystic Fibrosis.* Minneapolis, Minn.: University of Minnesota Press, 1991.

Wills, Christopher. *Introns, Exons, and Talking Genes.* New York: Basic Books, 1991.

ARTICLES

Arias, Ron. "A Medical Breakthrough Gives New Hope to David Reitz—And All Kids with Cystic Fibrosis." *People* (September 11, 1989), pp. 84–85, 89.

Barinaga, Marcia. "Knockout Mice Offer First Animal Model for CF." *Science* (August 21, 1992), pp. 1046–47.

Collins, Francis. "Cystic Fibrosis: Molecular Biology and Therapeutic Implications." *Science* (May 8, 1992), pp. 774–79.

Davies, Kevin. "The Search for the Cystic Fibrosis Gene." *New Scientist* (October 21, 1989) pp. 54–58.

Davies, Kevin. "Cystic Fibrosis: the Quest for a Cure." *New Scientist* (December 7, 1991), pp. 30–34.

Jacoby, Jack. "A Determined Doctor, Both Healer and Patient, Wages a Lifelong Struggle Against Cystic Fibrosis." *People* (September 24, 1990), pp. 67–70.

Kolata, Gina. "Genetic Defects Detected in Embryos Just Days Old." *The New York Times* (September 24, 1992), pp. A1, B10.

McNeil Pharmaceutical. "Living With Cystic Fibrosis: Family Guide to Nutrition." 1990 booklet.

Plummer, William, and Giovanna Breu. "A New Breath of Life." *People* (July 6, 1992), pp. 116–23.

Purvis, Andrew. "Laying Siege to a Deadly Gene." *Time* (February 24, 1992), pp. 60–61.

Silberner, Joanne. "Following the Blueprint of a Deadly Inherited Disease." *U.S. News & World Report* (November 4, 1991) p. 73.

Wolmuth, Roger. "Jimmy the Greek Faces His Longest Odds in a Family Fight for Life." *People* (October 26, 1981), pp. 28–31.

INDEX

Pages in *italics* indicates illustrations.

Adenosine triphosphate (ATP), 83, 84
Al-Awqati, Qais, 67
Amiloride, 83, 84
Amniocentesis, 21
Anderson, Dorothy, 12
Antibiotic treatments, 39–42, 86
ATP, 83, 84
Avery, Shiloh, 78

Beall, Dr. Robert J., 80, 85, 88, 93
Boucher, Richard C., 65, 83, 84, 87
Bronchiectasis, 32

Carter, Dr. Barrie, 93
CFF, 14, 80, 85, 86
CFTR protein, 70–71
Chest physical therapy (CPT), 36, 38
Clubbing, 32, *33*
Collaborative Research, 68

Collins, Francis, 65, 68, 75
Columbia University, 67
Cor pulmonale, 34
CPT, 36, 38
Crystal, Dr. Ronald G., 81, *82*, 83, 90, 91, 92
Cystic fibrosis
  and alternate birthing options, 74
  and antibiotics, 39–42, 86
  and coughing, 41–42
  diagnosis, 34, 36, 53
  ethical problems, 76
  and exercising, 38–39
  and fat intake, 47, 51
  and the heart, 33, 34
  in males, 16, 53
  medications for, 38, 43
  and salt intake, 53
  symptoms of, 18–19
  testing for, 19–21, 46
  in unborn babies, 21
  in women, 54
Cystic Fibrosis Foundation (CFF), 14, 80, 85, 86, 93

Deford, Alex, 72
Deford, Frank, 72
Deoxyribonuclease (DNase), 81, 83, 89
Diabetes mellitus, 50, 51
DiSant'Agnese, P. A., 12
DNase, 81, 83, 89

Endocrine glands, 16
Enzyme supplements, 47–48
Exocrine glands, 15, 44, 54

Fanconi, Dr. Guido, 12
Fost, Norman, 75, 76
Frizell, Raymond, 66

Gardner, Phyllis, 83
Gastrointestinal system, 45
Genentech Inc., 81
Genetic plans, 59–60
Genzyme Corp, 84
Glucose intolerance, 51
Gordon, Christine, 22
Gordon, Jacquie, 22

Hemoptysis, 33
Heredity
    and alternate birthing options, 74
    patterns of, 60–64, 62, 63, 75

Ibuprofen, 86
ICI Pharmaceuticals, 86
Immunication, 41

Immunoreactive trypsinogen test (IRT), 21
IRT, 21

Jacoby, Jack, 9
Jacoby, Jamie, 9
Juengst, Eric T., 76

Knowles, Dr. Michael R., 83, 84
Kyphosis, 56

Lifespan, average, 14
Lung transplants, 78, 79
Lungs, *17*, *25*, *26*

Malabsorption, 44, 46
Meconium ileus, 50

Nasal polyps, 32
National Center for Human Genome Research, 76
National Heart, Lung and Blood Institute, 81, 90
National Institutes of Health, 93
Nucleotides, 84

Pancreas, *13*, 44
Pneumothorax, 32
Polyps, nasal, 32
Protein delivery, 84–85
Pseudomonas aeruginosa bacteria, 29, *31*
Pulmozyme, 83

Quinton, Paul, 66

Rectal prolapse, 50
Reproductive system, 53–55, *54*, *55*
Respiratory system, *23*
Riordan, Dr. John R., 65, 68, 70

Secretory Leukoprotease Inhibitor (SLPI), 85, 86
Shak, Steven, 81
Sinusitis, 29
SLPI, 85, 86
Snyder, Jamie, 57
Snyder, Jimmy "The Greek," 57, 58
Snyder, Joan, 57
Snyder, Stephanie, 57
Spirometer, 34, *35*
Stanford University, 83
Staphylococcus aureus bacteria, 29, *30*
Sweat glands, 19, 52–53
Sweat test, 19, 21
Synergen, 86

"Thumps," 22, *37*
Tobramycin, 86
Triphosphate nucleotides, 84

Tsui, Lap-Chee, 65, 68

University of Alabama, 66
University of California, 66
University of Cincinnati, 93
University of Iowa, 66
University of Michigan, 65, 68
University of North Carolina, 65, 83, 86, 87, 92, 93
University of Utah, 68
University of Washington, 86
University of Wisconsin, 75
Upjohn Company, 86
Uridine triphosphate (UTP), 83
Ursodeooxycholic acid, 86
UTP, 83

Vanderbilt University, 93
Verlinsky, Yury, 21
Vitamin supplements, 48

Welsh, Michael, 66
White, Ray, 68
Wilfond, Benjamin, 75, 76
Williamson, Bob, 68